Julia Goddard

Wonderful Stories from Northern Lands

Julia Goddard

Wonderful Stories from Northern Lands

ISBN/EAN: 9783744750387

Printed in Europe, USA, Canada, Australia, Japan

Cover: Foto ©Andreas Hilbeck / pixelio.de

More available books at **www.hansebooks.com**

WONDERFUL STORIES

FROM

NORTHERN LANDS

BY

JULIA GODDARD

AUTHOR OF

'THE BOY AND THE CONSTELLATIONS' 'KARL AND THE SIX LITTLE DWARFS'
'MORE STORIES' ETC.

WITH AN INTRODUCTION

BY THE

REV. GEORGE W. COX, M.A.

and

*Six Illustrations from Designs by W. J. Weigand
Engraved by G. Pearson*

LONDON

LONGMANS, GREEN, AND CO.

1871

AUTHOR'S PREFACE.

ALTHOUGH English children have long been delighted with the legends of Germany and Scandinavia as collected in the ' Household Stories ' of Grimm, and in Dasent's ' Popular Tales from the Norse,' no use has yet been made of the materials of the Eddas and Sagas of Northern Europe for the amusement and the instruction of the Young. In the belief that these materials may be presented in a form as delightful as that of the old stories with which all are familiar, I have clothed a few of the Edda and other narratives in language which, I trust, the youngest child may understand with ease, and from which even they who have left childhood behind them may derive some enjoyment.

CONTENTS.

LIST OF ILLUSTRATIONS.

INTRODUCTION.

AMONG the marvels of the inchanted land of Folklore none is greater than the freshness which every
form retains, although it may be presented to us in
a hundred different dresses. We may see and feel
that under all these disguises we are looking on the
same being ; but we are never tired of listening to
the tale of his adventures, slightly as these may be
varied in each of the many versions of his history.
The repetition never wearies us: the monotony
never becomes irksome. Even when by long
acquaintance with some of these tales we know
what is going to happen in others, we read or listen
for the thousandth time with the feeling that
whether for old or young these stories can never
lose their charm. The child to whom is told the
old Greek tale of Psychê and Love,—how she was
carried away to a cave in a lonely garden, where
her sisters told her that she was wedded to a

hideous monster, how by their evil counsels she rose up in the night to look at her lover, how Love wakened by a drop of oil from her torch vanished away in the form of a dove, how Psychê sought for him in all lands and found him again at last after achieving three marvellous tasks,—will say at once, This is the story of Beauty and the Beast, or something very like it. But neither the child's wonder nor his delight will be lessened when he reads in Grimm's story of the Soaring Lark, how the youngest of three daughters whose father had to go a long journey, would have him bring her a singing, soaring lark; how he found the bird on a tree near a splendid castle, and how, as he was going to take it, a lion sprang from behind and said that he should never have it unless he promised to give him his daughter as his wife; how, when she had been wedded, the loathly lion became at night a beautiful prince who told her that no ray of light must fall upon him; how after a while at the marriage of one of her sisters a ray pierced through a chink of the door and fell like a hair line upon the prince, who in the same instant that it touched him was changed into a dove; how when the dove flew away she sought him for seven years, and then, aided by the Sun, the Moon, and the North wind, she found her husband in the power of a monstrous caterpillar; how the maiden attacked the huge insect which turned into a woman and again carried the prince away on the back of a griffin ; and how, when the prince was to be married to her enemy, she was suffered to enter his room first for the golden robe which the Sun gave her, and then for the golden hen and chickens which had been the gift of the Moon, and how on the second night the prince awoke and found by his side the maiden who had sought for him over the wide earth. The child, as he reads, knows here that the maiden is Psyche, and that in the end she shall meet him whom she has lost ; but he is none the less pleased when he sees the same beautiful form in the more homely dress of the Gaelic tale, which tells how the Daughter of the Skies * married a dog who at night became a splendid man, and when he discerns the magic gifts of the Teutonic bride in the wonderful shears, needle, and clue which are made the means of winning back the lost love of the Gaelic maiden. When he has read further the tale of the Twelve Brothers, of the Little Brother and Sister,

* Campbell, ‘ Popular Tales of the West Highlands,’ i. 282.

of Hansel and Grethel, of the Six Swans, and of
Little Snow White in Grimm's 'Household Stories,'
he will begin to feel that there is a whole family of
legends in which a maiden has a beautiful lover on
whom she is not suffered to look, while a jealous
mother or jealous sisters insist that the lover is
hideous, and tempt her to look at him while he is
asleep. In all he will discern the same machinery
bringing about the same result,—the dropping of
the burning liquid, the change of the man into the
bird, the weary wandering and the joyful reunion
after the accomplishment of superhuman tasks.
Soon perhaps he may find that there is another
group of legends in which the parts are inverted,
and in which it is the bride who is snatched away,
while the bridegroom has to seek her through many
a weary year. Turn where he may, the same
images will meet his eye: and the beings who love
and suffer in the Norse tale of East of the Sun and
West of the Moon,* are the beings whose joys and
sorrows are told again in the Hindu legend of
Urvasî and Purûravas,† in the Deccan tale of the

* See the tale in Dasent's 'Popular Tales from the Norse,' and
the poem so intitled in Mr. Morris's 'Earthly Paradise.'
† Max Müller, 'Chips from a German Workshop,' ii. 114, &c.

Rakshas' Palace,* in the True Bride and in the story
of the Drummer, in Grimm's collection.† He may
now be able to take these stories to pieces, and
to trace each feature through groups of other tales.
Thus, in Grimm's story, the prince shut up in the
Iron Stove answers to the maiden Brynhild imprisoned within the walls of flame on the Glistening
Heath, while the little toad which helps the princess
is the Frog Prince who brings back the golden ball,
the bright orb of the Sun, to the Dawn maiden who
has suffered it to fall into the water. Of course
the princess has to wander in search of the tenant
of the Iron Stove, and to serve like Cinderella as a
kitchen-maid ; of course she too has three nuts (the
gifts of the little toad), from which she draws forth
garments more brilliant than silver or gold, and of
course she wins back her lover just like the maiden
in the story of the Soaring Lark.

We have thus in our hands the clue which may
guide us through the mazes of folklore stories to
fountains of delight which can never be drained
dry. It may be impossible, perhaps, to bring back
the precise feeling which these stories may severally

* Frere, ' Old Deccan Days,' p. 205, &c.
† ' Household Stories.'

have inspired in those who knew but few of them; but even young readers at the present day will probably have devoured not only the ' Household Stories' of Grimm, and the Norse Tales of Dasent, but the West Highland legends of Campbell, the Deccan Tales of Miss Frere, the Icelandic legends of Powell and Magnüsson, and many more. That all these stories exhibit the same elements, he must soon discover. It is well that he should learn to draw pleasure from sources which will never fail him, and withal grow wiser as he recognises old friends under new forms in the legends of Greeks and Hindus, of Norwegians, Germans, Spaniards, and Englishmen.

Not a few of these old friends will be recognised in the stories gathered in this volume from the Eddas and other sources of Northern folklore. There may be repetition, but there is no sameness; and the common joys and sorrows which these tales reveal, impart to them an indescribable charm. Many, if not most of them, bring before us that great tragedy of nature which has stirred the hearts of poets in all countries and in all ages. Gods and men all mourn the absence of the bright being without whom life and gladness seem alike to be lost. In the story of Balder (II.) we have, in Bunsen's words, 'the tragedy of the solar year, the murdered and risen god, ' 'familiar to us from the days of ancient Egypt,' and ' of equally primeval origin here.' * When the gods stand round him as the end draws nigh, and shoot their arrows at him, we have the story which the Greeks told of Sarpêdôn, the chief of the far-off Eastern land, who in one version is brought to life again like Balder, like Osiris, and like Memnon, the glistening Son of the Dawn. But nothing on earth can hurt Balder, except one little plant of whom Odin thought it not worth while to exact the oath sworn by all other creatures. In other words, he can be slain only in one way, as Achilleus and other heroes are vulnerable only in one part; and thus his death comes from his blind brother, the darkness which slays the summer sun when the nights begin to get longer than the day. But the day of vengeance soon comes, and he is avenged by his young brother Ali or Wali, whose birth marks the gradual rising again of the sun after the winter solstice, until Balder the Beautiful once more reigns in Ganzblick or Breidablick, the abode

* 'God in History,' ii. 458.

of pure light, as Zeus dwells in Lykoreia, the mountain of light, and the sun god treads the shining path of Lykosoura. The same thought marks the story of Christin's trouble (VIII.) ; and in Christin we have the lovely Eurydikê who is snatched from her lover as soon as she becomes his bride. Orpheus in the Northern tale has become Sir Peter, but the change scarcely goes beyond the name. Like Orpheus, he seizes his golden harp, which is to rescue her from the ugly sprite who represents Hades or Polydegmon in the Greek story. When he strikes the chords for the third time, a white arm is raised above the surface of the water. It is the arm of Christin. As he goes on playing, Christin lifts her head above the water; but wiser than Orpheus, he takes care that his bride shall be on firm land before he ceases from his task. The gradual rising of Christin leads us to Grimm's story of the Nix of the Mill-pond, where the parts are again reversed, and the bride is seeking to rescue her lost lover from the waters. The spell of Orpheus and Sir Peter lies in this story in a golden comb, a flute, and a spinning-wheel. When the maiden plies her comb, his hand appears: when she touches the flute, his head is seen ; when she comes with the wheel, he leaps from the water and once more stands by her side.

Still more striking is the story of Iduna, whose golden apples are the apples of the Hesperides, which in Grimm's tale of the Old Griffin have the power of instantaneously restoring to health the King's daughter. Iduna is, in short, the beautiful maiden whose capture by the giant Thiasse is the stealing away of Persephonê from the plains of Enna by the terrible Hades or Polydegmon. In each case all nature feels her loss, and gods and men mourn because all strength and joy and beauty are taken from the face of the earth. The flowers refuse to bloom, the seed will not grow, the trees will not put forth their leaves, while the maiden remains in the dark land, and the mourning mother grieves at Eleusis until her child comes back. Then the joy of Bragi, like that of Dêmêtêr, is greater than the sorrow which has happily passed away, and thus in Bunsen's words we have here a story which 'is an exact counterpart of the earliest myth of Herakles, who falls into the sleep of winter and lies there stiff and stark till Iolaos wakes him by holding a quail to his nose.' * Iduna too comes back in the

---

* 'God in History,' ii. 488.

shape of a quail, the bird of spring, the quail Artemis who has her home on the Ortygian island. This return of the stolen or captive maiden is one of the subjects to which the imagination of the North was most powerfully attracted. We have it in Grimm's story of Rapunzel who is imprisoned in the dismal tower, to which the lover ascends on the ladder made by her golden hair, the golden locks which are stolen away from Sif (V.) by Loki, and restored after a while more beautiful than ever. We have it in the story of the Dwarfs,* in which the maiden, like Persephonê, eats a golden apple and sinks a hundred fathoms down in the earth, where the prince finds her with the nine-headed dragon on her lap. We see her again in the princess who lies seemingly dead in the House of Wood,† which breaks up in the spring like the ice. There is no mistaking the sudden thaw at the end of a Northern winter, as we read how the ' sides crack,' ' the doors were slammed back against the walls, the beams groaned as if they were being riven away from their fastenings ; the stairs fell down, and at last it seemed as if the whole roof fell in.' In the beautiful palace, in which the princess on becoming con-

* Grimm.   † Ibid.

scious finds herself, we see the loveliness which the earth puts on, on the sudden outburst of spring.

The image of Iduna is but a reflection of that of Ingebjorg in the story of Frithiof (XIII.), who is deprived of his chosen bride as Bragi is despoiled by Thiasse (X.). Here the enemy whose wife Ingebjorg becomes, while Frithiof is gone to the Orkneys, is old King Ring, who appears in a more sombre and less kindly guise in the old Rink-rank of the German story,* and in the Troll in the legend of the Old Dame and her Hen in Dasent's collection.† Ingebjorg here becomes the wife of Frithiof's enemy; but in other respects there is very little difference between his story and that of Odysseus (Ulysses). Like the chieftain of Ithaka, he comes back to find his home spoiled and his wealth gone; like him, he returns in mean disguise (as do Boots and the Princes in scores of German stories) ; like him he is recognised by his dog, and jeered and flouted by the courtiers, until one who ventures to lay hands on him receives forthwith the punishment of Arnaios or Iros in the Odyssey. Like him, when he throws off his mean dress, he appears in all

---

* Grimm.   † ' Popular Tales from the Norse.'

the radiant beauty of youth, for Athênê, the Dawn maiden, can make men young though twenty years of toil and sorrow may have passed since they had left their homes. Of course, Ring dies, and Ingebjorg becomes at last the wife of Frithiof, as Penelope is at last restored to Odysseus.

But Frithiof has a magic ship Ellide, which knows his will and obeys his bidding; and this ship is none other than the patient ox in the story of Olaf the Saint (XII.), whose word makes the slow brute bound like a stag and fly with the swiftness of an eagle. These ships are the same as Skidbladnir, the magic bark of Freya, which can hold all the Æsir and can yet be folded up like a kerchief; the iron-boat in the story of Big Bird Dan,* which 'moves if you only say, Boat, boat, go on ; ' the ships of the Phaiakians which have neither helm nor rigging, but which, veiled in mist, visit every city and corn-field in the earth. The clouds can move where they will, and without helmsmen or rowers they never fail to reach their destination; and so no harm can befall the fleet of Alkinoös or the good ships of Frithiof and Olaf.

In the stories of Christin (VIII.) and Iduna (X.),

* Dasent, ' Popular Tales from the Norse.'

we have seen beautiful maidens shut up in the heart of the earth.   In the story of the giant Thrym (I.) it is Thor's magic hammer which is stolen away and buried eight fathoms deep.   On this hammer, as on the presence of Iduna, the power of the Æsir depends.   In the version here followed, Thor goes to the dwelling of Thrym disguised as a woman, an incident which vividly recalls similar scenes in the Greek stories of Theseus, Dionysos, Odysseus and Achilleus.   But it was also told that the hammer came back of itself, rising one mile in each year for eight years, till it reaches once more the abode of Thor.   Like this hammer, the Glass Coffin* rises through the floors of ice to the upper air, and the case, when opened, expands into a magnificent castle.   Like this hammer, too, the brazen hammer in the Greek story takes nine years to descend from the earth into the lowest depths of Tartaros.

The vein of quiet humour and familiarity with the highest gods is a prominent characteristic of Northern stories. This humour passes into seeming irreverence in the stories of the Master Smith,† but

---

* Grimm, ' Household Stories.'
† Dasent, ' Norse Tales.'

it is not peculiar to the folklore of Northern Europe.
The tricks of Loki the god of the fire are the tricks
of the Greek Hermes, the Master Thief who steals
cattle when he is six hours old, and then going back
to his cradle in the guise of a babe calmly says that
he knows not what kind of things cows are ; * nor is
Thor himself (IV.) more genial and rollicking than
the Greek Herakles in many of the stories related
of him.   There is close kindred again between Loki
and the fire-god Hephaistos, the Latin Vulcanus,
who are reflected again in Völund (III.), (the Way-
land Smith of Sir Walter Scott's ' Kenilworth,') who
has a beautiful Valkyrie wife, as in the Iliad the
lovely Charis is the wife of the limping Hephaistos,
the youngest of the gods.

   The wonderful quern in the story of Frothi (VI.)
is one of a vast number of vessels which are inex-
haustible sources of wealth.   It is, again, a quern
in the Norse tale ' Why the Sea is Salt ; ' but the
same thought is presented in the horn of Amal-
theia, in the can or pail of the milkwoman in the
Hindu story of Sûrya Bai,† in the horn of Oberon,
and the cauldron of Ceridwen.   It is, in short, the

* ' Tales of Ancient Greece,' p. 23.
† Frere, ' Old Deccan Days.'

huge cauldron which Thor got for the giant Oegir
(Ager) (XI.), and whose savoury contents went spon-
taneously to each guest as he might wish for them.
It is the goblet of Tegan Euroron, the dish of
Rhydderch, the basket of Gwyddno, the table of the
Ethiopians to which no good thing is ever lacking,
the lamp of Allah-ud-deen,* who has only to rub
it and get all that his heart may desire.

In the chaining of Fenris (IX.) the wolf is the
great enemy of the Æsir, and his kinsfolk are the
great serpent Jormungand and Hela the ghastly
goddess of death.   He is the evil beast who is to
devour the moon when the twilight of the gods has
come: meanwhile, he finds occupation in swallow-
ing maidens or goats, for he is the wolf who eats
Little Red Cap† or Red Riding Hood, and swallows
the six little goats in the German story.‡

The story of Thorvald (VII.) has been sug-
gested by a beautiful feature in the mythology
which relates to the land of the Æsir.   The
search for the foundation of Bifrost, the rainbow
bridge of Heimdall, the lord of Himinbjorg, the
city of heaven, is that yearning of the soul for a

* 'Arabian Nights.'
† Grimm, 'Household Stories.'
‡ Ibid. 'The Wolf and the Seven Little Goats.'

beauty unattainable on the earth, which finds expression in the Christian legend of the Monk and
the Bird,* whose singing, like that of Hjarrandi in
the Gudrunlied can make a hundred years seem
as but a moment.

Scarcely less powerful than the spell of Hjarrandi
is the charm of these stories, which delighted the
common forefathers of Danes and Germans, Norwegians and Englishmen, Franks and Icelanders.
We stand before a palace with a thousand doors,
in which each room reveals wonders at once old
and new; and, if I mistake not, the key, which
with these few words I place in the reader's hand,
will enable him to wander at will through an
enchanted abode beautiful as the Ganzblick in
which Balder dwelt, for it does indeed bring before
us the wonderful works of God, as they appeared to
the minds of men and women like ourselves, who
lived in the fresh childhood of the world.

G. W. C.

* See the poem of Archbishop Trench.

WONDERFUL STORIES.

———◦◦⟨⟨⦚⟩⟩◦◦———

I.

HOW THOR RECOVERED HIS HAMMER.

THOR was a mighty god. He ruled the summer-
heat and raging thunder, and none among the
Northern gods was more powerful than he. His
beard was red as gold, and he wore a crown of
twelve stars. His eyes flashed lightning when he
went forth to battle, and the sound of his chariot-
wheels echoed through the heavens. Greater was
his palace than any ever built by man, and its
halls gleamed as with the brightness of fire.

Strongest of all the gods was Thor, and as if he
had not strength enough in himself, it fell to his
lot to own three things which made him so mighty
that none might withstand him: his belt of power,
which gave him double strength whenever he

B

girded it on; his iron gloves; and the wonderful hammer Miölnir.

This marvellous hammer was as much coveted by the other gods as it was prized by Thor, since no evil could befall him who possessed it. But if Miölnir should fall into the hands of the Jötuns or giants, Thor would lose his power and the Jötuns would reign in Asgard.

Asgard was the beautiful country of the good gods—who were called Asi—smiling and fertile, with green pastures, clear broad rivers, wild hunting-grounds, and fruits and flowers such as no child of earth has ever seen; whilst Jötunheim, where the giants lived, was a bleak desolate land with barren mountains and scarcely a tree or flower. Hence it was not strange that the giants should wish to change their dreary country for the blooming kingdom of Asgard.

Amongst the Jötuns was a powerful king whose name was Thrym. He was lord of the Thursi—the cold, shivering Thursi who knew not what warmth was. Very gloomy was the region over which Thrym reigned, and wherever he went cold and wretchedness followed in his train.

He was a shaggy-looking giant with wrinkled

brow and furrowed cheeks, and hair and beard as white as snow. His hands were hard and cold as ice, and his touch alone would freeze the blood in a man's veins. He was quite as cold as his shivering people, which is not to be wondered at, since in the land of the Thursi there is no summer. It was winter, bleak winter, all the year round.

Now Thrym, in his dreary home, often longed to have the beautiful Asgard for his kingdom; and once he was very near getting it; for, whilst Thor lay in a heavy sleep, Thrym seized his wonderful hammer, and hid it away.

Great was the wrath of Thor when he awoke and found his hammer gone. He was a little frightened too; that is, as frightened as it was possible for so great a god to be. But he was far more angry than frightened; for how should a Jötun dare to take the hammer of Thor?

His anger was hot within him, and yet he must not show it, for it would go ill with him if everyone should know of his loss. Some of the Jötuns, wiser than Thrym, might take advantage of it, as Thrym would certainly have done had he known the value of his prize.

Thor therefore calmed himself, and, after pondering for awhile, he called to Loki, the lord of the mighty fire, and told him what had happened. And when they had taken counsel together, they agreed to go to Freyia and ask her to help them.

Freyia was the lovely wife of Oder. Her eyes were bluer than the blue forget-me-not, her complexion fairer than lilies and roses, her teeth were like pearls in a setting of coral, and her hair like glittering threads of gold.

'What dost thou want of me, O mighty Thor?' asked Freyia.

'I want a robe with wings that will carry the wearer round the world,' answered Thor. 'The giant Thrym has stolen my hammer, and I must get it back without delay.'

'Thou shalt have a robe, and that speedily,' returned Freyia, 'though it should be woven with silver and gold.'

For Freyia knew how needful it was that Thor should win back his hammer, and forthwith she brought forth from one of her great brazen-clasped chests a shining robe, with wings that flashed and sparkled in the sunlight.

Thor took it very thankfully, and giving it to

Loki, said, 'Now put it on and fly away to Thrym, and bid him to give me back Miölnir, lest I come in wrath and take terrible vengeance upon him.'

Then Loki donned the shining dress, highly pleased to find that the sparkling wings moved so easily that they would bear him through the air like a bird; and he answered cheerily, 'No fear! No fear! I will bring Miölnir home with me.'

And away he flew; and the moving of the silver wings made a pleasant noise like the clashing of sweet-toned cymbals; and Thor watched him flashing along like a shooting star until he was lost in the distance.

On, on he flew, swifter than the wind, on towards Jötunheim.

Thrym was seated upon his throne, a great mound of snow, frozen so hard that the Thursi had carved it into the form of a chair. And Thrym was making collars for his dogs, and combing his horses.

As Loki drew near, the king of the frost-giants stopped in his task, and, looking up, said, 'How are you, Loki, and what brings you to Jötunheim?'

Now Thrym knew quite well why Loki had come, but he wished to hear what he would say. . .

'The gods are full of anger because you have stolen Thor's hammer,' replied Loki; 'and they will not be appeased until you have given it up again.'

'That is a likely thing,' returned Thrym. 'Why should I give it back when I have had the trouble of taking it? If they will give me something in exchange, then I may perhaps think about it.'

'What do you want?' asked Loki.

Thrym considered for a moment, and then he said, 'You see that I am very dull and lonely here, in spite of my being king. I should be much happier if I had a wife, and I can't find anyone among the Jötuns to suit me. Now, I have never seen anyone so beautiful as Freyia, and Freyia I must have for a wife.'

'Freyia!' shouted Loki—'Freyia, the wife of Oder?'

'Yes, Freyia,' answered Thrym, quite calmly. 'And no one shall have Thor's hammer unless Freyia comes hither to be my bride.'

'Freyia!' repeated Loki, for he was too much surprised to say anything else.

'Yes, Freyia,' said Thrym once more. 'I have stowed the hammer away safely. It is hidden eight fathoms deep under the ice and snow, and unless you bring Freyia with you, you need not trouble yourself to come here again.'

And Thrym went on combing the tangled mane of one of the horses; and as he combed it, he hummed a song—at least what sounded like a song to him, but if you had heard it you would have thought it a peal of thunder.

After he had combed the mane to his pleasure, he whistled to one of his dogs. And if you had heard him whistling, you would have supposed it to be the great north-wind warring and blustering as though it would tear up the giant oaks.

A great fierce dog came bounding up in answer to the summons, and Thrym fitted one of the golden collars round his neck.

After which Thrym looked up at Loki.

' Why are you waiting ? ' said he ; ' you had better fly away with my message to the gods. Tell them, If Thor wants his hammer, he shall have it as soon as they send Freyia to me.'

Loki knew that there was no use in further words. The giant Thrym had made up his mind, and nothing that he could say would alter it.

So, spreading out his wings, he sped again to

Asgard, to tell the gods how ill he had fared with his errand.

On his way to the palace of Oder, he met with Thor.

'What is to be done?' asked Thor, when he had heard what Loki had to tell him.

'We must take counsel again with Freyia, and see if she can help us.'

Together they went to the palace.

'How have you prospered?' asked Freyia.

'But ill,' replied Loki; and then he told her what had befallen him with Thrym.

The roses in Freyia's cheeks turned crimson as peonies when she heard what Thrym wanted, and her blue eyes shot forth flames like fire. She stamped with rage, and paced wildly up and down the marble floor. How should the beautiful wife of Oder become the wife of the Jötun Thrym?

'You should have taken better care of the hammer,' said she to Thor. 'Do you think that I am going to leave Asgard just to please you? Thrym may keep Miölnir for all I care. I will never be queen of the Thursi. I tell you I will not go.'

'If you do not go, we shall all have to leave

Asgard together,' replied Thor; 'for it will soon be noised abroad that Thrym has stolen my hammer, and the Jötuns will come at once and seize our beautiful country, and no one can hinder them.'

Then all the gods who had been waiting for Loki's return began to urge first one thing and then another; and as no one liked to have his counsel set aside, they all waxed fierce and shouted at one another, until there was such an uproar that it was quite impossible to hear anything that was said; and all the time Freyia was pacing up and down, tearing her hair and weeping, and saying again and again that she would never be the bride of the Jötun Thrym.

I do not know how long this state of things would have lasted, had not a very wise god, named Heimdall, stepped forward to say how they might win back Thor's hammer, though Freyia should yet remain in Asgard.

' Let us dress Thor in Freyia's garments,' said Heimdall. 'With Freyia's silken robes, and bright necklace, and a long veil over his face, he may deceive Thrym, and win back the hammer himself.'

'That will do, that will do,' shouted the gods, all excepting Thor.

'That will do,' cried Freyia; 'the thought is good.'

But Thor did not think it good, and his wrath at the counsel was even greater than the rage of Freyia had been. The walls of the palace shook as he strode up and down the great hall, and he waved his arms about so fiercely that the other gods were fain to keep out of his way, since a blow from the heavy hand of Thor would have smitten them to the ground. But the crafty Loki crept near to him and whispered, 'Nay, Thor, be not angry. Think yet again. Heimdall has not spoken unwisely. Something must be done, and that right quickly, if the gods are to reign yet in Asgard. If your hammer is not forthwith brought back, we shall have the Jötuns upon us before we are aware; and then all will be over with the Asi, and they must, sorrowing, depart from this land of joy and beauty.'

'What! am I to be dressed as a woman?' thundered Thor.

'It is only a wise trick to enable you to act as a man and a god,' returned Loki. 'What matters it if, for once in your life, you put on a flowing veil and glittering ornaments? It is better than to be

banished from your home, or, worse still, to be a
slave to the Thursi.'

Thus spake Loki, till at last Thor suffered himself to be dressed as a bride. His hair was braided
and hung with jewels, Freyia's necklace was placed
round his neck, while her keys dangled at his belt.
And over all the tiring maidens flung a long veil of
shimmering silver-gauze. Truly he looked a very
stately bride, a head taller than most of the Asi ;
but then you must remember that Thrym was a
giant, so that by his side Thor would not look so
large.

Well pleased that he had thus prevailed with
Thor, Loki made ready the chariot drawn by two
strong he-goats, and he and Thor stepping into it,
they set off upon their journey.

The mountains shook at the rumbling of the
chariot-wheels, the earth trembled, and the great
oaks bent their heads ; for all things knew that
Thor, the son of Odin, journeyed along, and that
he was in terrible wrath.

Soon there was a stir throughout the land of the
Thursi. For Thrym had heard the panting of the
he-goats, and had called to his people and said,
' Up, up, ye Thursi ! stir yourselves, make ready a

feast, and prepare for merry doings. My bride cometh from the land of Asgard. Up, up! and greet her loyally.'

And the Thursi roused themselves, and the feast was spread in the banqueting-hall. Great barrels of mead; oxen and sheep roasted whole; huge salmon, and savoury cates, all mighty in size, as became the greatness of the Jötun Thrym.

And Thrym, king of the Thursi, listened eagerly. Louder and louder sounded the whirring of the chariot-wheels. Swiftly the chariot drew nearer, for the he-goats sped too fleetly to touch the ground. Thrym could see it now—a small speck far away in the blue distance. Soon he could discern the polished horns of the goats shining in the sunlight, and the showers of glittering sparks and flashes of fire that played around the chariot. Nearer—nearer. And then was heard a roar of many voices shouting, 'Welcome to the wife of Oder! Welcome to the beautiful Freyia! Welcome to the bride of Thrym !'

Thor's wrath burned within him, but Loki twitched his veil and besought him to curb his anger, whilst Thrym, stalking through the frost-giants, stepped forward to hand out the bride from

the chariot. But Loki glided in between them.
'Let me lead the bride into the banquet,' he said.
'None must speak to her until after supper.'

And Loki led Thor to the festal board, whisper-
ing as he went along, 'Do not betray yourself too
soon.'

Thor was scarcely in the humour to take counsel
from anyone; nevertheless he remained silent, and
moodily seated himself at the table.

The Thursi looked admiringly at the splendid
figure, covered with sparkling jewels that shone out
hazily through the flowing veil. The king himself
gazed with delight, for he believed that he had won
a right fair bride, and had humbled the pride of
the Asi.

She can eat well, too, thought he, as the bride
devoured a full-grown ox and eight salmon, and
drank three firkins of the frothing mead.

'What a hungry maiden!' quoth he in an under-
tone.

Loki heard it, and, leaning forward, answered,
'Her appetite is great, O Thrym! for she hath
neither eaten nor drunk for eight long days, so
much hath she desired to see thee.'

Then Thrym, king of the Thursi, felt pleased,

and, when supper was over, he lifted the veil to give the bride a kiss.

The tiring maidens had painted Thor's face with white and red to look like a woman's; but they could not take away the fierce glitter of his eyes, that gleamed more fiercely than ever now.

Thrym started back. 'Her eyes seem on fire,' he said.

But again the crafty Loki put in his word. 'Ah! she hath had no sleep for eight long nights, so much did she long to see thee.'

Then again was the foolish Jötun well pleased, and called for his sister to come and greet the beauteous princess from Asgard.

And when she came, and beheld the golden rings and armlets that Thor wore, she said, 'If thou wouldst win my love, give me of thy jewels.'

But Thor made no reply.

Then said the king of the Thursi, 'Bring out Thor's hammer; so shall we fulfil our word. A bride as fair as Freyia is well worth its ransom.'

The heart of Thor was full of gladness when Miölnir was laid before him. He could scarcely keep down his joy, but it was not yet time to show himself.

He waited till Thrym drew near to take his hand in token of betrothal ; then up he sprang, and brandishing the hammer high above his head, he shouted, 'I am Thor!'

And down he struck the giant to the earth, with so fell a blow that Thrym lay dead at his feet.

Next he set to work to slay all the giants who had taken part in the feast, and, this done, he turned and slew the Jötun's sister who had asked him for bridal gifts.

Then, as there were no more Thursi to kill, he said quietly to Loki, 'Make ready the chariot, that we may return home.'

And as they drove along, lo! everything was changed: the mountains shook not, neither did the forest trees tremble, for there flashed no fire forth from the chariot-wheels, which rolled smoothly and noiselessly over the ground. The dark clouds fled away, the hills burst into verdure, the earth was hung with garlands of flowers, and the tall pines raised their crests proudly, as though they would touch the heavens.

Thor had won back his hammer, and was returning in triumph to Asgard, and his power and glory were felt throughout heaven and earth.

II.

THE STORY OF BALDER.

BALDER'S DREAMS.

ODIN, the king of the Asi, had many sons. Thor was the eldest and bravest, but Balder was the best and the most beautiful. His hair was bright as the sunshine, his eyes shone as the stars of heaven, and no flower of earth was so fair as his smooth white brow. His voice was sweet as the murmur of running waters, and the words he spoke were so full of wisdom that the Asi were never tired of listening to them.

Truth reigned in his heart, and no evil thought ever found entrance there. All the gods loved Balder, and his praises sounded throughout Asgard.

He had a fine palace in the broad heavens, called Breidablik, into which nothing evil might enter ; and on its pillars were carved Runic rhymes that had the power of giving back life to the dead.

Balder had a wife named Nanna, who loved him tenderly, and they dwelt in all happiness together.

Quickly the days flew by as Balder and Nanna loitered among the pleasant groves and gardens, listening to the song of the birds, and gathering the fruits and flowers that never failed nor faded, for in the country of the Asi there was always summer.

But suddenly, in the midst of his happiness, came to Balder dark dreams, which filled him with a secret fear that danger was nigh at hand.

' What aileth thee ? ' asked Nanna, who saw that her husband's step was not light, as it was wont to be ; that his voice had a mournful tone ; and that his eyes were full of sadness.

' Dreams that I cannot understand come to me night after night,' said Balder ; ' I cannot forget them.'

' Dreams are idle things,' answered Nanna ; ' Balder should be wiser than to care about them.'

But when she looked at Balder's anxious face, she too began to feel frightened ; and she told her fears to the Asi, and when they heard of Balder's dreams, they also were afraid.

Then Balder went to his mother.

He found her weaving with her maidens in one of the many halls of Odin's palace.

' O mother Friga ! is there aught to fear in these dreams of mine ?' asked Balder.

C

And Friga listened whilst he told her of the dark visions that came to him night after night; but she replied not to his question, for she knew that the dreams foretold death.

'I will talk with thy father,' she said. 'Now hasten back to Nanna and comfort her. Tell her that Odin is all-wise, and will be able to turn aside evil from thee.'

Yet after Balder had departed, the queen sat down and wept, for her heart was very heavy.

Must Balder the Beautiful indeed die?

Odin found her still weeping when he returned from hunting. She was so full of grief that she did not hear his footstep, and when he laid his hand upon her shoulder she started with fear; for she was dreaming of death, and thought that the hand of Death lay already heavy upon her.

Then she told Odin of Balder's dreams and asked, 'O Odin, shall our son indeed die? Can nothing be done to save him?'

Odin looked sad as he made answer, 'If all things were loving to him as we are, then could no ill befall him.'

And Friga said, 'Thou canst command all things. Let all things take an oath that they will not hurt Balder. Let us go through the world ourselves and see that this is done. There is nothing that can withstand the king and queen of heaven.'

THE OATH.

The sun rose upon the palace of Odin, the famous Valhalla, whose ceiling was formed of glittering spears, roofed in with golden shields. Over the benches of the great hall were strewn coats of mail of cunning workmanship, while armour and weapons of war were piled on every side.

The king and queen and all the Asi were gathered together.

And Odin spoke: 'O Asi, will ye swear to do no harm to Balder?'

And the voices of the gods sounded like a burst of glorious music as they answered, 'We swear!'

And Odin spoke again, 'I ask ye, O spears and arrows, poisoned barb and pointed javelin, sword, shield, and weapon of every kind, that ye take an oath to do no harm to Balder.'

And a fierce clash rang through the splendid hall. For so the weapons answered back their lord and master.

And forth from the mighty palace, through the outer courts, through the broad roadways, through one of the five hundred and forty gates through each of which eight hundred warriors might march abreast, the king and queen went forth into the world—alone, and on foot, for they went on an errand of love, and not on a journey of state.

First, of the dazzling sun did Odin take an oath, that neither in his noon-day heat, nor in his rising beams, nor in his setting rays, would he ever do hurt to Balder.

And every cruel beast that prowled for prey, and every harmless beast that roamed the earth, the treacherous snake and the hideous worm, swore that from them no harm should come to Odin's son.

And every bird that twittered on the boughs, the soaring eagle and the keen-eyed hawk, and every creeping thing, and every humming insect, and every fish that swam in shallow rivers swore to the king and queen that they would do no hurt to Balder.

And every giant tree of the forest, and every bending bush by the river-side, every reed that sighed, and every twining plant that crept over the earth, swore that no harm should come through them to Balder.

And every flower lifted up its perfumed blossoms as Friga bent over them, and softly swore the oath, even before she asked them ; and the rich ripe fruit, that glowed all yellow and purple and crimson, echoed the words of the gods.

Through forest, through meadow, through fallow land, on they went to the shores of the great ocean ; and the waves reared their crested heads and roared back, 'We swear,' in answer to the prayer of the king of heaven.

Up rose the whale, the glittering dolphin, and the shark, and all the tribe of fishes and sea-monsters, and swore to do no hurt to Balder.

The mighty rocks trembled as they heard the shout, and they too swore to do him no harm.

The winds awoke when Odin called upon them, and wailed and shrieked, 'We swear, we swear !'

And the clouds rolled together, and from their midst the thunder pealed, 'I swear;' and the forked lightning sealed the oath.

Then Odin and his wife turned their steps towards the vast cities dotted over the world, and all the people took the oath. And pale Sickness and wasting Famine came forth to meet the king, but, before he suffered them to go back to their lurking-places, he had made them swear that their hands should never touch the form of Balder.

Swiftly the king and queen then travelled on-wards—swiftly, as only the gods can travel. And the sun went down in the heavens, and the evening dews fell, and the moon and stars shone out in the night sky.

And from the rimy dew, and from the moon and stars, did Odin take an oath, even from the night itself, that its dark shadows should never hurt Balder.

Odin and his wife were in the snow-regions now, and the great ice-blocks sparkled in the moonlight; and ice and frost and snow and hail and thaw swore faithfully to do no harm to Balder.

And still the king and queen of Asgard jour-neyed on. The way was cold, and the moon was hidden behind the clouds; but huge fires were burning on either side, to light them on their way. And from the fire that leaped and twisted and roared like a living creature, did Odin take an oath that neither fire nor heat should ever injure Balder.

Then the king and queen sat down to rest, for

their work was done. All things had sworn to do no harm to their son, and Balder henceforth need fear no evil.

Everything had sworn but one small twig, that seemed to Odin and his wife too young and tender to take an oath from. It was too weak to hurt anyone.

So the king and queen rose up with fresh strength, and went back to their own land. And Balder's dreams were thought of no more, and all went well with him.

Now, since the oath had been taken, the Asi often amused themselves with shooting arrows at Balder, or throwing spears, or hurling stones, as he stood for a target; and none could wound him, since wood and iron, stone and poisoned barb had sworn the oath to do no harm to Balder.

LOKI'S TRICK.

But Loki, the lord of fire, was very angry when he found that no harm happened to the good Balder.

'How is it,' he asked, 'that nothing can hurt Balder?'

And answer was made to him:

'All things have sworn an oath that they will do no hurt to Balder.'

Then was Loki still more wroth. Why should all things swear such an oath? Why should Balder be safe from all harm? It was only an idle story that the Asi were telling him; he would not believe that it was true.

And he determined to find out for himself all about it from Friga. Therefore he made himself look like an old woman, because he knew that if he went in his own form the queen would not speak to him.

And first he praised up Balder, and said how good and beautiful he was, and what a great thing it was that everything in the world had promised not to hurt him. He must be greatly loved by all.

'Yes,' said Friga, 'the work was easily done. Everything loved Balder and was willing to take the oath.'

'Everything?' said Loki, in wonder.

'Everything,' answered the queen, 'that is, everything except one poor little twig that grew upon an oak planted eastward of Valhalla—a slender sprout called mistletoe ; it was so weak that it was not worth while to take an oath from it.'

'Yes ; it was quite useless,' said Loki. And he went away,—but not home. He bent his steps to the oak that Friga had spoken of, and there he found the little twig grown into a strong bush, with pliant green boughs and pearly berries.

Carefully he cut the plant away, and carried it off to Niflheim, the home of the Mist, where, in a secret room of his palace, he fashioned the straightest and strongest branch into a sharp arrow.

He dared not use any feathers, for the feathers would not have carried it against Balder, so he split the fibres as fine as it was possible to split them, and made them so like feathers that one could scarcely have told them from real ones. And when it was done he made a present of it to Höder, one of Balder's brothers.

Now Höder was blind, and therefore could not see who had given him the arrow, or perhaps he might have suspected mischief.

THE SHOOTING MATCH.

Outside the gates of Valhalla there is a wood called Glasir. In this wood the leaves of the trees are all of red gold.

Here the heroes who have fallen in battle on earth, and have been taken to Asgard, amuse themselves with fighting and slaying each other afresh, but they always come back to life at breakfast-time. When they care no more for this sport, they hunt the wild boar Schrimner, upon whose flesh they feast at eventide; but in the morning they find him alive again, and ready for another day's hunting.

Here, in an open space, were the gods assembled for a shooting match, and Balder stood ready to serve as a mark for them.

Beautiful he looked, with folded arms, still as a statue. His fair hair flowed over his shoulders, and his blue eyes were placid as a blue lake when the wind has gone down.

Nanna, his wife, was there, and Friga and all her court, to see the shooting.

Each tried his skill.

Some hit Balder, and others missed the mark; but of those arrows that struck, none harmed him.

Last came the blind Höder. Strong he was, and his skill in shooting was wonderful.

'Welcome, good brother,' cried Balder; and Höder aimed his arrow in the direction of the voice.

Once, twice he shot.

'Well done! thou hast hit the mark,' said Balder, laughing; 'blind men have better eyes than those who can see.'

Then Höder fitted his third arrow to the bow. It was one that Loki had given him.

'Take steady aim, good Höder,' said Balder, and again, guided by the voice, Höder drew his bow.

The arrow whizzed through the air. It struck Balder, and, with a sudden cry, he fell.

'I die! I die!'

Quickly was Balder raised up, but it was of no avail. The light had gone out of his blue eyes, and his arms hung powerless. Balder was dead!

'Balder is dead! is dead!' echoed through the wood.

'Dead! Nay, who hath broken the oath?' cried Odin, as he rushed forward.

And Friga followed him, and leaning over her son, strove to call him back to life.

Nanna held Balder's head on her lap. 'Hush!' she said, 'he only sleeps, he is not dead; all things have sworn that they will do no harm to Balder.' And she tenderly drew the arrow from the wound.

Friga took it, and, looking carefully, she saw that it was made of the wood of the slender twig that grew on the oak eastward of Valhalla.

Then she knew at once that there had been treachery. She remembered the old woman. 'It is Loki,' she said, 'who has done this.'

FRIGA'S COUNSEL.

Odin's grief was very terrible. Balder was so good, so greatly beloved. What would the Asi do without Balder?

And the mourning throughout the land of Asgard was very bitter. It was as if the sun had set for ever since Balder was gone.

At length Friga roused herself. 'Why should we give up hope? Perhaps we may be able to win back Balder. Hela is not always cruel; it may be that she will give up him who has fallen by crafty wiles into her hands.'

But Odin shook his head. 'Balder is too fair a prize for Death to give up.'

'At least we may try,' answered Friga. 'Who,' she asked, 'amongst the Asi is bold enough to ride to Hell and ask Hela tò give us back our beloved Balder?'

Then stepped forward Hermöd, another of Odin's sons. 'O mother Friga, I will ride to Hell, and see whether I may not win back our brother Balder.'

'Up, then! There is no time to lose; the journey is long and the path is rugged. Hasten away, and we will perform the funeral rites, so that there may be no hindrance on that score.'

Then was Odin's horse Sleipner saddled, and the brave Hermöd mounted him and rode away.

Now the horse Sleipner had eight legs, and his speed was as the speed of the wind.

BALDER'S FUNERAL.

Then the Asi made all things ready, that the body of Balder should receive due honours; and they gave command that it should be carried on board his own ship Ringhorne, and that then the funeral pile should be raised.

The good ship Ringhorne lay upon the beach, fast driven on the sand; and when the Asi strove to move her, not an inch could she be stirred.

'It needs a giant to do this,' said the Asi.
And they sent to Jötunheim.

Soon came the giantess Hyrrocken, riding upon
an enormous wolf; her reins were vipers, and she
brought four berserks to hold the wolf when she
alighted.

She went straight to the shore, and going to the
prow of the vessel, gave it one push.

Straightway from the rollers on which it was
raised, fire shot forth, the earth shook, and the ship
glided into the water.

Thor was wroth at this, for it seemed too much
like his own power over the lightning, and he
would have killed the giantess had not the other
gods besought him for her.

The funeral train was a very long one: Odin,
with his ravens Huginn and Muninn; Friga and
the Valkyries, the goddesses of slaughter, who
waited on Odin, each with her glittering spear and
proud unmoved countenance; Frey, in a chariot
drawn by Gullinborst, the golden-haired boar
that drew the sun-god's chariot round the world;
Heimdaller, on the horse Guldtopp; and all the
Asi in their brightest array. The one-eyed
Hrimthursi were there, and the mountain-giants

had come from their barren homes, for Balder was loved by every one far and near.

Upon the funeral pile was placed the favourite horse of Balder and his riding gear.

At the last the body of the beautiful god was laid there also, and Odin took a torch and lighted the pile. The flames sprang quickly up, and into the flames he cast Balder's ring, Dröpner.

Higher, higher flashed the fire. Soon would the body of Balder be quite burnt up.

Wild was the mourning of the Asi; and they bowed their heads and cried, 'Woe! woe! for Balder the Beautiful is snatched from life. Cruel Death holds him in her cold arms. Woe! woe! for there is none among the Asi like unto Balder the Fair!'

As for poor Nanna, the wife of Balder, she had died of grief.

HERMÖD'S RIDE.

Now when the brave Hermöd mounted Sleipner, he let the reins hang loose, so that the swift steed might feel no curb. And on and on, faster than the flight of the swiftest eagle, he galloped along.

Nothing stayed him. Over hill, through valley, lake, and river, the horse Sleipner dashed without once stopping.

Then the skies grew darker, but it was not the darkness of night. He was drawing nigh to the regions of Hela, the regions trodden only by the dead. Nine days and nine nights he rode through deep dark valleys, so dark that he could not see where he was going.

'On, Sleipner, on!'

And Sleipner paused not, but thundered through the deep valleys, whose silence was broken only by the sound of the horse's hoofs.

'On, Sleipner, on!'

Darker grew the valley, blacker than midnight; on galloped the horse and the rider—a flash of lightning across the valley of thunder.

'Whither, O Sleipner, whither dost thou bear me?'

There is a dark river whose waters are blacker than pitch and almost as thick. Across it is thrown a bridge overlaid with gold. It is the bridge Gyall, and none but the dead pass over it.

Out came Modgunn, the maiden who keeps the bridge.

'What is thy name?' she asked.

'Hermöd, the son of Odin.'

'Five companies of dead men have crossed the bridge,' she said, 'but it rang under no step but thine. Thou hast the look of the living, not of the dead; wherefore dost thou follow in their path?'

'I ride to Hell to seek for Balder. Tell me, hast thou seen him?'

'Yea, he hath passed the bridge. Over the bridge Gyall he came. If thou wouldst follow him, take the road northward; that leads to Hell.'

On galloped Hermöd.

And long did Modgunn hear the clattering of Sleipner's hoofs in the distance. Darker and harder became the path; but Sleipner thundered on. Nine days and nine nights had he galloped without resting, yet neither rider nor horse was weary.

At length they reached the fence that surrounds the palace of Hela. But there was no entrance for the living.

And Hermöd saw that the fence was high, and that every gate was locked and barred, and the air was so heavy that he could not raise his voice loud enough to make anyone hear.

D

'On, Sleipner, on !'

And Sleipner pricked up his ears and with one bound cleared the fence, and Hermöd was at the door of Hela's palace.

HELA'S DECREE.

Hermöd found the palace door open, and he walked in and wandered through many rooms and passages until he came to the great hall, where he found Balder in a place of honour.

There too he found Hela, and he told Hela how the gods grieved for the death of Balder, and besought her to let Balder go back to Asgard.

' The king offers anything he has for a ransom.'

' Nought that the king has would be of any worth to me,' said Hela; 'what are the treasures of the living to the dead ?   I covet nothing that Odin owns.'

But Hermöd was not daunted, and he still besought Hela to find a way for Balder to return to life.

Then Hela thought for awhile, and after deep pondering, she said : 'I have heard that Balder is greatly beloved. If he is so beloved that everything in the world weeps for him, then may he go back to Asgard; but if one single thing refuses to weep for him, then must he remain with me for ever.'

Then Balder came near and said: 'I give thee my thanks, O Hermöd, that for my sake thou hast ridden on this perilous journey. If I should not come back, tell Odin to keep the ring Dröpner in memory of me, and tell Höder not to grieve, since my death was no fault of his.'

Then he gave the ring Dröpner to Hermöd, and the ring had a strange power, for every ninth night it brought forth eight rings like itself, because it had passed through the fire on Balder's funeral pile.

Nanna too came near and sent gifts to Friga, and a gold ring to Fulla, the queen's handmaiden.

And Hermöd remounted Sleipner, and rode away from Hell.

WHO WILL WEEP FOR BALDER?

The Asi listened day after day for the sound of Sleipner's hoofs.

Day after day Friga went up to the topmost tower of the palace, but Hermöd was not in sight.

'Heimdall, Heimdall! canst thou not yet hear him?' she asked. For Heimdall's ears were sharper than those of the other Asi, so sharp that he could hear the wool growing on the backs of the sheep, and the tender blades of grass springing up in the meadows. But Heimdall could hear only what was going on in the upper world, his hearing could not pierce the regions of Hela.

At last Heimdall spoke: 'Hermöd has reached the upper world; I hear the hoofs of Sleipner strike the ground.'

Then Friga took her station upon the watch-tower, so that she might catch the first glimpse of the rider. Perchance he might bring her beloved Balder back with him.

'Is he very far off, Heimdall?'

'Three thousand leagues away; yet never fear, Sleipner runs like the wind, and he will soon be here.'

Friga waited a little, then again she looked forth.

'I see a speck, a tiny speck. Can it be Hermöd?'

Then Heimdall looked forth and listened eagerly. 'It is Hermöd!'

'Is he alone?'

' He is alone. But one rider touches the panting sides of Sleipner.'

Then the queen wrung her hands, and went down into the great hall to await with the king and the Asi the coming of Hermöd.

Through the wide gates, and up the stately avenue, the rider came. He scarcely waited for his steed to stop before he sprang from the saddle. He dashed up the broad steps into the palace, and there was a great cry: 'What news, O Hermöd?'

Then Hermöd told how Hela had decreed that if all things in heaven and earth should weep for Balder, then might he come back to Asgard.

Then Friga took courage again, for she knew how much Balder was beloved.

And the bidding went forth, 'Let everything weep for Balder.'

And all around were sighs and lamentations. There was not a dry eye among the Asi; the tears rolled down to the beard of Odin, and even Thor wept. Höder had never ceased to weep, and all things wept, showing the sorrow of the gods.

The clouds burst into gentle showers, the earth was bathed in dew, the air was dimmed by the veil that the dewdrops threw over it, and the moon and the stars grew pale from sorrow.

And beasts, and birds, and trees, and flowers, all mourned, there was nothing in heaven and earth that wept not.

'Surely he may come back,' said Friga, 'for all have wept for Balder.'

'All?'

Then came a messenger who had been sent forth to see if there was anyone who did not weep. His face was pale and grave, and he looked as one who bore heavy tidings.

The queen approached him anxiously.

And thus spake the messenger, 'There is a giantess named Thöck. She doth not weep for Balder's death. She sits and mutters, "Neither in life nor yet in death, did Balder give me gladness. Let Hela keep her prey."'

Then Friga threw herself on the ground, and wept, for she knew that Balder would never come back to Asgard.

And Odin also knew that hope was at an end. Moreover, he believed that the giantess Thöck was none other than the evil envious Loki.

THE RETURN OF BALDER.

But not for ever will Friga weep for Balder, not for ever will Odin mourn his son, not for ever will Hela keep her prey, for the day is at hand, nay is even now come, when the gates of her dreary kingdom shall be unlocked, and she shall no longer hide in darkness those who are born to light.

A gentle breeze is blowing over a country more beautiful even than Asgard, a new sun is shining. The corn is springing from unsown fields, the flowers are bursting into blossom on every side ; laughter and joy and sweetest strains of music resound over the plains of Ida, and there rises a glorious palace, the palace of Gimli, more splendid even than Valhalla. There the Asi have assembled in peace once more, for the dark days of Ragnarok have passed away, and Surtur has purified the world with fire.

A train moves slowly over the plain, and at its head are seen two who move like kings— Balder the Beautiful and his brother Höder whom Vali the avenger slew. Him Balder had welcomed to the dreary home of Hela and soothed his grief and bid him not despair, for he had learned the wondrous runes that told how Hela should in time set all her prisoners free.

And so the brothers waited and hoped for the day of freedom, and the scales fell from Höder's eyes, and he was no more blind. He looked upon Balder, and the two loved one another better even than in the olden days, for sorrow and captivity bound them closer together.

Over the plains of Ida moves the train. Nanna is there, and many a long-imprisoned one; and as it advances the Asi standing around the throne of Odin send forth a shout that rends the air: 'All hail! all hail! Hail Balder the Beautiful!'

And Friga clasps her long-lost Balder in her arms, and all her grief is swept away in that ecstasy of joy.

Joy for ever and ever; for nevermore can harm happen to Balder. He will dwell with those he loves for ever in the halls of Gimli. And Friga has ceased to weep, for she has regained her long-lost son.

III.

THE STORY OF VÖLUND.

THERE was once a king of Finnland who had three sons, all eager lovers of hunting. The two elder were named Slagfin and Egil, the youngest was called Völund.

But Völund not only loved hunting like his brothers ; he had a power which his brothers did not possess. He was a wonderful craftsman at the forge, and could make arrow-heads, spears, and weapons of all kinds. Moreover, he could model shields with rare chasing, and sometimes would fashion chains and armlets of fine gold that the daintiest queen might be proud to wear.

So well he loved his work that he spent more than half his time at the forge, and never gave it up but for a day's hunting with his brothers. And more than once he even gave up the chase, for though he loved hunting well, he loved his anvil better. And his workshop was quite a sight to see with all the wonderful things that he had made hanging round.

At last Slagfin said to Egil, 'Völund spends too much of his time at the forge, it is not work befitting a king's son. He will lose all interest in the chase, unless something is done to rouse him.'

And Egil replied: 'Thou hast spoken well, my brother, and a thought has come into my mind. I am growing tired of the hunting grounds near home; the sport is not so good as it used to be. But far away in Ulfdal, on the shores of Ulf lake, is a mighty forest. There we may chase the wolf and the wild boar, and in the lake we may catch more fish than we shall know what to do with. Let us go thither and take Völund with us. Then will he forget his forge and his bellows, and live as a king's son ought to live.'

The idea pleased Slagfin greatly, and away he went to Völund to propose the plan.

He found Völund at work upon slender spears of a new pattern. 'Ha!' he said, as he took one of them up to look at, 'we could make good use of this at Ulfdal. What do you say to going there with Egil and myself? We might build a hut on the borders of the lake, and live upon the game we kill. You have been toiling at your forge too long, the change will do you good.'

'I must finish this spear first,' returned Völund, 'it is the best of the lot, and though it is so light, it is so strong that nothing can blunt its point or break it in twain.'

'Work away, then,' said Slagfin, 'but be ready to start with Egil and myself by to-morrow's dawn. You must bring your choicest weapons with you, for we expect rare sport.'

'Take any you please,' answered Völund, 'for I have no time to choose for you. The spear I am working upon will suffice for me, I shall want no other weapon.'

Then Slagfin chose out arrows, and sharp spears, and hooks, and strong chains, long nails and a heavy hammer.

'We must build for ourselves,' he said, 'for no man dwells on the borders of Ulf lake.'

'So much the better,' responded Völund; 'I like the sound of my hammer, and the song of the birds, better than the voices of men.'

And Slagfin went away well pleased that Völund was willing to go to Ulfdal. And early in the morning, just as the sun was rising over the low hills, the three brothers were seen loaded with their hunting gear, starting off for the wild forest that bordered the lake.

Völund was strong and mighty of limb; he had muscles almost as strong as those of Thor, his eyes were dark, and his black hair curled crisply round his brow. He was not so handsome as his fair-headed brothers, but he was taller and more like a king, and everyone said as he passed along, 'There is no one in Finnland to equal Völund.'

Further and further they left the city behind, wilder grew the country and the sun shone high above them.

'Shall we not rest?' asked Egil; 'we have journeyed many a mile and my limbs are weary; besides, it will be pleasanter travelling when the sun goes down.'

Then Völund smiled : 'If you were accustomed as I am to the heat of the forge, you would not mind the sun's rays. Nevertheless, let it be as you please,' he added throwing himself down at the foot of a tall pine tree; 'there is no hurry for getting to Ulfdal, the game will not chide our loitering, since it will give them longer life in the forest.'

So the three brothers rested and after awhile set out again on their march. There remained yet three days' journey to Ulfdal. But at length they reached it, and were repaid for their toil when they saw the tall pines shoot up their branches high into the air, and heard the low growl of the wolf not far off, and beheld the blue lake stretching out like a quiet sea with the wild swan sailing on its glassy waters and the water-fowl rustling among the reeds and rushes.

' This is a pleasant place,' quoth Slagfin.

Then the brothers heaped together a pile of boughs and brushwood and made themselves a fire. And Egil fitted an arrow to his bow and shot the sea-fowl as they lazily fluttered by, whilst Slagfin cast a net into the lake and hauled up a plentiful supply of fish.

Meanwhile the strong Völund had cut down several pines and built up a hut so quickly that Slagfin and Egil thought it had been done by magic.

It was but a rude hovel for the sons of a king, but what did the princes care? The summer sun shone brightly and the nights were warm, and besides they loved hunting well enough to care little for all discomforts.

They spent their time in the forest, and many a wolf-skin would they have to carry back to Finnland. Many a wild boar fell under the spear of Völund, and there was great slaughter among the water-fowl and the wild-deer.

Day after day went by, and Völund rejoiced so much in the great free forest that Slagfin and Egil hoped that he had forgotten his forge.

One morning when they went forth from the hut they marvelled at hearing voices in the distance; and not the voices of men, but low sweet tones and gentle laughter, such as they were accustomed to hear from the queen's ladies at court.

And lo, close by the water's edge there sat three fair maidens spinning flax. And as they span they sang a song that even to Völund sounded sweeter than the notes of the forest birds.

The brothers drew nearer, and never had they seen faces so fair as those of the three maidens, who were so busily engaged in their task that they did not see Völund and his brothers until they were close to them.

When however they did see them, they seemed in no whit abashed, but began to talk to them, and to tell them how they too had heard of the quiet

Ulf lake and had determined to leave their own country and abide on the outskirts of the wild forest.

'So we put on our swan-coats and flew away,' said the maidens, 'and the king, our father, knows not what has become of us.'

When Slagfin heard that the damsels were king's daughters he was very glad, for he had already fallen in love with one of them.

So also had Egil, and so even had Völund, and by good luck each had chosen a different princess. There was no need of quarrelling in the matter, and it was soon arranged that the three princes should marry the three princesses and that they should all remain in Ulfdal together.

For a long time everything went on well, and they were all very happy, and Völund and his brothers would have been content to live for ever in the forest with their beautiful wives. They went out hunting together, and Völund had built up a forge and he made all sorts of ornaments for his wife and her sisters.

But it happened that the sisters grew tired of the life they were leading. Though Völund and his brothers did not know it, their wives were

Valkyries, who loved war better than anything else, and so they became weary of the pleasures of hunting and longed to go to battle again. And one day when their husbands were absent they put on their swan-coats and flew away.

When the brothers came back and found that their wives had left them they were in great trouble, and Slagfin and Egil determined to stay no longer in Ulfdal, but to seek through the world for their lost princesses. But Völund resolved to stay where he was, hoping that perchance his wife might come back to him ; and he continued to make armlets and necklaces and delicate chains to please her when she should return. But alas! she never came back.

And after a time it came to pass that Nidad, King of Sweden, heard tell of Völund and how he could make all sorts of armour and weapons and trinkets. And Nidad sent a band of armed men to Ulfdal, who took Völund and brought him to Sweden.

There he was obliged to work at the forge for the King's pleasure, and to make swords of sharpness and shoes of swiftness, and other marvels for the king and his people. And Völund was very angry and several times sought to escape.

Then the queen counselled Nidad to cut the sinews of Völund's legs, so that he should be unable to walk and might remain with them always.

And when this was done Völund was put on the island of Sjoa-stad, where he was obliged to work day and night with scarcely any rest.

Völund was very wroth at being thus cruelly treated, and determined upon revenging himself; but it was a long time before he was able to do so. He was lame and could not move about, and he grew very weary and began to languish. At last two of the king's sons came to him, and with bitter taunts bade him make two swords, sharper than any he had yet made; and Völund's wrath was roused yet more, and he rose up and slew the two young men, and of their skulls he made drinking cups which he sent to the king, and of their teeth a breast jewel for the queen. And the king and queen admired them greatly, little knowing how they had been made.

Soon the king's sons were missed, and search was made for them, but they were not to be found.

Long mourned the king and the queen; but Völund kept his secret, and worked on at the forge.

One fine morning when he was toiling at a shield which the king had bidden him make, the king's only daughter came to ask him to make a ring and a chain of gold for her.

She was very fair, fairer even than his Valkyrie wife, and she spoke in a gentle tone to Völund, for she felt the more sorry that he had to work so hard, because she knew he was the son of a king.

And Völund gazed eagerly upon her, and her soft voice was like music to his heart. He promised to make a ring and a chain of gold more beautiful than any she had ever seen, and the princess went away well pleased, promising to come for them in two days.

The two days seemed very long to the princess, for she was eager to see what her ring would be like, and she wanted to see Völund again, for she pitied him greatly.

To Völund the time went more quickly, for he had work to do, and the chain and the ring were only just made when the princess came for them.

She was delighted when she saw them, for never

had anything been so delicately wrought in Sweden.

And Völund threw the chain around her neck, and gently put the ring on her finger, and then he sighed.

'Why do you sigh?' asked the princess.

'For my sorrows,' replied Völund.

'Ah, you wish to go back to your own land,' said the princess; 'I do not wonder at it, for it is sad to be a captive.'

'Until two days since I wished to return,' answered Völund, 'but not now—unless, indeed,' he added, 'you would go with me and be Queen of Finnland.'

The princess made no answer, but Völund knew that she was not angry, for there was a smile upon her lips.

And after she was gone, Völund began to work away at something that he had not thought of before, and that was not in the way of his trade. He made two coats of feathers, so light that they would rise into the air of themselves; and the next time that the princess came he asked again if she would fly away with him and be Queen of Finnland.

Still the princess made no answer, but she took a ring from her hand and gave it to Völund and then went away, and Völund knew that before long he should fly home to his own country.

Again came the princess and again Völund asked her if she would fly away with him and be Queen of Finnland.

And the princess took up one of the feather coats, and without saying a word drew it over her dress. Then Völund put on the other coat and they rose up high into the air.

King Nidad and his queen were sitting on the terrace in front of the palace when Völund and the beautiful princess floated by.

The king shouted loudly, 'Ah, traitor! thou art carrying away my daughter. Out, archers, out and shoot him.'

And Völund answered: 'I have revenged myself for thy cruelty to me. Thy sons have I slain, and from their skulls hast thou drunk the sparkling wine, and the queen wears their teeth in her shining breast jewel. And now do I take thy daughter from thee, since she loves me better than she loves thee.'

Then higher, higher, rose Völund and the

princess into the air, and soon they were out of sight.

There were great rejoicings in Finnland when Völund alighted at the palace, for the old king was dead, and Slagfin and Egil had not yet come home from searching after their wives, and the people had no one to reign over them.

So Völund reigned over Finnland, and ruled his people wisely and well. Nevertheless he loved his forge better than ruling, and all his spare time he worked away at his smithy, and may be working there yet if one could only tell where to find him.

IV.

THOR'S ADVENTURES AMONG THE JÖTUNS.

ONCE upon a time Thor set out upon his travels, taking Loki with him, for despite Loki's spirit of mischief he often aided Thor, who doubtless, in the present expedition, felt that Loki might be of use to him.

So they set off together in Thor's chariot drawn by the two strong he-goats, and as night drew nigh, stopped at the hut of a peasant, where they asked food and shelter.

'Food I have none to give you,' said the peasant, 'I am a poor man and not able even to give supper to my children, but if you like to rest under my roof you are welcome to do so.'

'Never mind the food, I can manage that,' said Thor, dismounting from the chariot and entering the hut.

It was a poor place, and not at all fitted to receive one of the Asi, but Thor was glad enough to meet with it, wretched as it was.

'You can kill the goats,' said he, 'they will make us an excellent meal.'

The peasant could not help thinking that it was a pity to kill two such fine animals; but wisely thinking that this was no affair of his, and that the stranger had a right to do as he pleased with his own, he set himself to obey Thor's orders, and with the help of his daughter Raska soon spread a savoury repast before the hungry god and his attendant.

'Sit down all of you,' said Thor, 'there is enough and to spare.'

So they all sat down, and the peasant and his children shared a more plentiful meal than had fallen to their lot lately. Thor and Loki also did ample justice to the food, and when supper was over the thunder-god bade the peasant gather the bones and place them in the goatskins, and making them into a bundle he left them on the floor until the next morning.

When the morning came and the early sun shone in through the crevices, Thor raised his hammer and instead of the bundle of bones the peasant and his son and daughter saw the two goats standing as fresh and lively as if nothing had happened to them, saving that one of them halted a little in his walk.

When they sought to learn why this should be, it was found that Thialfe, the boy, in getting the marrow out of one of the bones, had broken it, and it was this that caused the goat to go lame.

Thor was very angry, and was very near killing not only Thialfe but also the peasant and his daughter Raska, but they begged so hard for their lives that he consented to spare them on condition that the boy and girl should follow him in his travels.

To this they agreed, and Thor, leaving the chariot and goats in the peasant's care, went on his journey, giving Thialfe, who was a very swift runner, his wallet to carry.

On and on they journeyed until they came to a great sea.

' How are we to get over this ? ' asked Loki.

' Swim across it,' replied Thor.

And in they all plunged, for Thialfe and Raska were used to a hardy life, and so were able to swim with scarcely more weariness than Thor and Loki, and were not long in reaching the opposite shore.

'The country does not improve,' said Loki

looking round upon the desolate plain that lay
outstretched between them and the borders of a
dark forest, which they could just see in the far
distance. One or two huge rocks thrust their
jagged points high into the air, and great blocks of
stone were scattered about, but there was no sign
of herbage and not a tree to be seen nearer than
the forest belt bounding the horizon. Heavy grey
clouds were drawing nearer and nearer to the
dreary earth, and twilight was fast approaching. 'It
looks not well, in good sooth,' answered Thor, 'but
we must push on and perhaps may find it better
as we go onward. Besides, night is drawing nigh,
and as there are no dwellings to be seen we must
try to gain the shelter of the forest before it is too
dark to see where we are going.'

So they pushed on, and though they looked to
the right hand and to the left soon found that they
were in a land where no men lived. There was
therefore nothing to be done but to quicken their
speed, in order to reach the shelter of the forest.
But though they strove to the utmost, the twilight
deepened into darkness and the darkness became
so deep by the time they reached the forest, that
they only knew they had arrived there by Loki's

striking his head against a low branch, and soon after this Thor cried out:

' Good luck ! I have found a house. Follow close after me and we will make ourselves comfortable for the night.'

For Thor in groping along had come to what he supposed to be a wall of solid masonry.

' Where are you ? ' asked Loki, ' for it is so dark that I cannot see you.'

' Here,' answered Thor stretching out his hand; 'take hold and follow me.'

So Loki clutched Thor's arm and Thialfe in turn seized the arm of Loki, whilst Raska clung to her brother and wished herself safe at home in her father's hut.

And thus they groped their way along the wall seeking to find an entrance to the house.

At last Thor found a huge entrance opening into a wide hall, and passing through this they turned to the left into a large room which was quite empty, and here, after eating some food, they stretched themselves upon the hard floor and wearied out with the day's march soon fell asleep.

But they did not sleep long, their slumbers were broken by a rumbling sound as of a coming earthquake, the walls of the house shook and peals of thunder echoed through the lofty chamber.

Thor sprang up. 'We are scarcely safe here,' he said, 'let us seek some other room.' Loki jumped up speedily, as did also Thialfe and Raska, who were in a great fright wondering what dreadful thing was going to happen to them. They willingly followed Thor, hoping to find a safer place.

To the right they saw another room like a long gallery with a huge doorway, and into this Loki, Thialfe, and Raska crept, choosing the furthest corner of it; but Thor took his stand at the doorway to be on the watch if any fresh danger should threaten them.

After a somewhat uncomfortable rest, Loki, Thialfe and Raska were not sorry to find that the day had dawned, though as there were no windows in the house, they only knew it by hearing the cock crow.

Thor was better off, for the doorway was so wide that the sunlight came pouring in without hindrance. Indeed the huge size of the doorway made Thor think that the builder must have given up all hope of ever finding a door large enough to fit into it.

He strolled away from the house, and the first thing that he saw was a huge giant fast asleep upon the greensward ; and now he knew that the thunder that had so frightened them in the night had been nothing more or less than the loud snoring of the giant.

So wroth was Thor at the thought that such a thing should have made him afraid, that he fastened on his belt of strength and drew his sword and made towards the giant as though he would kill him on the spot.

But the giant opening his great round eyes stared so steadily at Thor, that the god became mazed and could do nothing but stare in return.

At last however he found voice to ask, 'What is your name?'

'My name,' said the giant, raising himself on one elbow, thereby causing his head to rise so high into the air that Thor thought it was taking flight altogether, 'is Skrymner; you I believe are the god Thor?'

'I am,' answered the god.

'Do you happen to have picked up my glove?' asked the giant carelessly.

Then Thor knew that what he and his companions had taken for a large house was only the giant's glove, and from this we may judge how huge a giant Skrymner must have been.

Thor made no answer, and Skrymner next asked whither Thor was travelling; and when he found that he was journeying to Utgard, offered to bear him company, as he too was going to the same place.

Thor accepted the giant's offer, and after eating a hearty meal, all were ready for another day's march.

Skrymner showed himself a kindly giant, and insisted upon carrying Thor's bag of meal, putting it into his own wallet, which he slung across his broad shoulders.

It must have been a strange sight indeed to see the great giant stalking along with his smaller companions at his heels; and we may well marvel how they managed to keep pace with him, or how Thor was able to raise his voice to such a pitch as to reach the giant's ears.

Nevertheless all went well, and they trudged cheerfully along, never flagging in their talk.

Once Skrymner took Raska on his shoulder, but the height made her so giddy that she was glad to come down again and walk quietly by the side of Thialfe.

When night overtook them they encamped under one of the great oak-trees, for they were not yet out of the bounds of the forest. Skrymner to judge by his loud snoring fell asleep the moment he lay down upon the ground, but Thor and his comrades were not so tired as to forget that they had tasted nothing since breakfast time. Accordingly they set to work to open the wallet that Skrymner had given into their hands before closing his eyes.

But it was no easy task, and with all their efforts they failed to open it. Not a knot could they untie, and their fingers were chafed and aching.

Neither were they more able to awaken Skrymner, and Thor's anger waxed exceeding fierce. 'You shall pay for this,' said he, flinging his hammer at the giant.

Skrymner half opened the eye nearest to Thor and said in a very sleepy voice, 'Why will the leaves drop off the trees?' And then he snored as loudly as before.

Thor picked up his hammer, and approaching nearer drove it into the hinder part of the giant's head, who again half waking up, muttered, 'How troublesome the dust is.'

Thor was exceedingly astonished at this, but thought nevertheless that he would once more make trial of his power ; so coming up close to Skrymner he struck with such force as to drive the hammer up to the handle in the giant's cheek.

Then Skrymner opened both eyes and lazily lifting his finger to his face said, ' I suppose there are birds about, for I fancied I felt a feather fall.'

Now was Thor fairly disconcerted ; and the next morning when the giant told him that they must now part as his road led him another way, he was by no means ill-pleased, and he let Skrymner go without so much as bidding him 'good speed.' Skrymner however seemed not to notice that Thor was glad to be quit of his company and gave him some very friendly advice before he left him.

' If you will take my advice,' said the giant, ' you will give up this thought of visiting Utgard. The people there are all giants of greater stature even than I, and they make nothing of little men, such as you are. Nay, more, you yourself are likely to fare but badly amongst them, for I see that you are rather apt to think too much of yourself and to take too much upon you. Be wise whilst there is time, think of what I say, and don't go near the city.'

' But I will go there,' shouted Thor, almost choked with rage; 'I will go in spite of all the Jötuns of Jötunheim. None shall hinder me, and the giants shall see and wonder at the mighty power of the god Thor.'

And as he spoke the rising sun fell full upon the city of Utgard, whose huge brazen gates glittered in the sunlight. Even though they were so far away, Thor could see how high they were, and as he drew nearer their vast size filled him with amazement ; but when he reached them his wonder was beyond all words, for he and his companions seemed no larger than grasshoppers, in comparison with their height.

The gates were not open, for it was yet early ; so Thor and his comrades crept through the bars and entered the city. As they passed along the streets the houses were so tall, that it was only by crossing to the opposite side of the broad road that they were able to see the windows in the topmost stories. And the streets were so wide that it was quite a journey across them.

Once a mouse darted out of a hole and Raska

screamed, for she thought it was a grisly bear. The mouse also shrieked and made much more noise than Raska, as well it might, for a cat so huge that Thialfe half thought it must be the monster of Midgard seized it, and giving it a pat with one of its paws laid it dead on the pavement.

As for the horses their hoofs were terrible to look at, and Thialfe and Raska must have climbed up ladders if they wished to see their heads.

The people were quite as large as Skrymner had described, and Thor and his companions were obliged to be very careful lest they should get trodden upon, as it was very doubtful if the people even saw them.

Still Thor walked along with the proud consciousness that he was the god Thor ; and feeling that though he was so small he was yet a person of some importance, made his way to the palace, and desired to see the king.

After some little time he and his fellow travellers were ushered into the presence of Utgarda Loke, the king of the country. And Utgarda Loke, hearing the door open, raised his eyes, thinking to see some great courtier enter, but he knew nothing of the bows and greetings of Thor, until happening to

F

cast his eyes to the ground, he saw a little man with his companions saluting him with much ceremony.

The king had never seen such small men before, and there was something so absurd to him in the sight, that he burst out laughing.

And then all the courtiers laughed also, pretending that they had not seen the little creatures before.

It was some time before they all left off laughing, but at length there was a pause, and Thor essayed to make himself heard.

'Though we are but small in comparison with the Jötuns,' said he, angrily, 'we are by no means to be despised, but are gifted with powers that may surprise you.'

'Really!' answered Utgarda Loke, raising his eyebrows. And then he and his courtiers laughed louder than before.

At last there was another pause in their merriment, and the king added: 'However, we are willing to give the strangers a fair trial in order to prove the truth of what their spokesman, whom I take to be the god Thor, says. How say you? What can this one do?' And he pointed to Loki.

'Please your majesty, I am very great at eating,' returned Loki.

'Nay,' answered Utgarda Loke, 'you must grow a little before you are great at anything.'

At which speech the courtiers again shouted with laughter; but Utgarda Loke, turning to his servants, bade them make trial of Loki's powers. So they brought a great trough full of food, and Loki was placed at one end, and a courtier named Loge at the other. They both fell to work to devour what was before them, and met at the middle of the trough. But it was found that whilst Loki had only eaten the flesh of his portion, Loge had eaten, not only the flesh, but the bones also. Therefore Loki was, of course, vanquished.

Then Utgarda Loke turned to Thialfe. 'And pray, in what may this youth be specially skilled?' he asked.

'I am a swift skater,' answered Thialfe.

'Try him,' said the king.

And Thialfe was led to a plain of ice, as smooth as glass, and one named Hugr was set to run against him. But though Thialfe was the swiftest skater ever known in the world, yet Hugr glided past him so fleetly that he had returned to the starting post before Thialfe had done more than a quarter of the distance.

Three times did Thialfe match his speed against Hugr, and, three times beaten, withdrew from the contest as disconsolate as Loki.

'And now may I ask what you can do yourself?' said the king to Thor.

'I can drain a wine-cup with anyone,' replied the god.

'Try him,' said Utgarda Loke.

And forthwith the royal cupbearer presented a drinking-horn to Thor.

'If you are as great as you pretend to be,' said the king, 'you will drain it at one draught. Some people take two pulls at it, but the weakest among us can manage it in three.'

Thor took up the horn, and being very thirsty took a steady pull at it. He thought he had done very well, but on removing it from his lips he marvelled to see how little had gone.

A second time he took a draught, but the horn was far from being emptied.

Again a third time he essayed to drain it, but it was full almost to the brim.

Therefore he set it down in despair, and confessed himself unable to drain it.

'I am disappointed in you,' said Utgarda Loke, 'you are not half the man I took you for. I see it is of no use asking you to do warrior's feats ; I must try you in a simpler way, in a child's play that we have amongst us. You shall try to lift my cat from the ground.'

Thor turned quite scarlet, and then became white with rage.

'Are you afraid ?' asked Utgarda Loke, 'you look so pale.'

And a large grey cat came leaping along, and planted itself firmly before Thor, showing its sharp claws and glaring upon him with its fiery eyes.

Thor seized it, but in spite of all his efforts he was only able to raise one of the cat's paws from the ground.

'Pooh ! pooh !' exclaimed Utgarda Loke, 'you are a mere baby, fit only for the nursery. I believe that my old nurse Hela would be more than a match for you. Here, Hela, come and wrestle with the mighty god Thor.'

And Utgarda Loke laughed disdainfully.

Forth stepped a decrepit old woman, with lank cheeks and toothless jaws. Her eyes were sunken, her brow furrowed, and her scanty locks were white as snow.

She advanced towards Thor, and tried to throw him to the ground; but though he put forth his whole strength to withstand her, he was surprised to find how powerful she was, and that it needed all his efforts to keep his feet. For a long time he was successful, but at length she brought him down upon one knee, and Thor was obliged to acknowledge himself conquered.

Ashamed and mortified, he and his companions withdrew to a lodging for the night, and in the morning were making ready to leave the city quietly, when Utgarda Loke sent for them.

He made them a splendid feast, and afterwards went with them beyond the city gates.

'Now tell me honestly,' said he to Thor, 'what do you think of your success?'

'I am beyond measure astounded and ashamed,' replied the god.

'Ha! ha!' laughed Utgarda Loke, 'I knew that you were. However, as we are well out of the city

I don't mind telling you a secret or two. Doubtless you will receive a little comfort from my
doing so, as you confess that your coming hither
has been to no purpose.

'In the first place, you have been deceived by
enchantments ever since you came within the
borders of Jötunheim. I am the giant you met
with on your way hither, and if I had known as
much of your power then as I do now, you would
never have found your way within the walls of
Utgard.

'Certainly I had had some slight experience of
it, for the three blows you gave would have killed
me had they fallen upon me. But it was not I,
but a huge mountain that you struck at ; and if
you visit it again, you will find three valleys cleft
in the rocks by the strokes of your hammer.

'As for the wallet, I had fastened it with a
magic chain, so that you need not wonder that you
could not open it.

'Loge, with whom Loki strove, was no courtier,
but a subtle devouring flame that consumed all
before it——'

Here Loki uttered an exclamation of delight,
but Thor bade him be silent, and Utgarda Loke
went on:

'Thialfe's enemy was Hugr or Thought, and let man work away as hard as he pleases, Thought will still outrun him.

'As for yourself, the end of the drinking-horn, though you did not see it, reached the sea, and as fast as you emptied it, it filled again, so that you never could have drained it dry. But the next time that you stand upon the seashore, you will find how much less the ocean is by your draughts.

'The grey cat was no cat, but the great Serpent of Midgard that twines round the world, and you lifted him so high that we were all quite frightened.

'But your last feat was the most wonderful of all, for Hela was none other than Death. And never did I see anyone before over whom Death had so little power.

'And now, my friend, go your way, and don't come near my city again, for I tell you plainly I do not want you there, and I shall use all kinds of enchantment to keep you out of it.'

As he ended his speech, Thor raised his hammer, but Utgarda Loke had vanished.

'I will return to the city, and be avenged,' said Thor.

But lo! the giant city was nowhere to be seen.

A fair pasture-land spread itself out around him, and through its midst a broad river flowed peacefully along.

So Thor and his companions, musing upon their wonderful adventures, turned their steps home ward.

V.

SIF'S GOLDEN HAIR.

SIF was the wife of Thor, and Thor was the son of
Odin.   Thor lived in a splendid palace which had
five hundred and forty halls.

Sif sat weeping bitterly as she gazed into the
stream that served her as a mirror.   Why should
she be so unhappy ? Surely it was a great thing to
be the wife of the god Thor, and mistress of a palace
with five hundred and forty rooms ; nevertheless
she wept, and good reason she had for doing so.

Sif had prided herself very much upon her long
golden ringlets, which were so beautiful that they
were praised throughout the land of Asgard.   Now
they were all gone, there was not a single hair left
upon her head.

Doubtless, the sight was strange, and had you
seen her you might have felt half inclined to laugh ;
but Sif thought it no laughing matter.   All her hair
was gone, and there were no wig-makers in Asgard
to supply her with new tresses.   So Sif was very

sorrowful. Besides, what would Thor think of her when he saw her? Would he know her for the beautiful Sif? and as she caught a glimpse of herself in the watery looking-glass her tears fell faster than ever.

Not far from the spot where she was sitting, there was a cavern, whose mouth was half hidden by a tall pine tree, and from behind this tall pine tree a dark face, whose eyes gleamed with malicious joy, peered forth. The more Sif wept, brighter shone the cruel eyes, and Loki (for it was he) laughed softly to himself.

Loki was at the present time at enmity with Thor, and to vex him he had charmed away Sif's beautiful hair. He was now making merry at her grief, and rejoicing in the thought of how vexed Thor would be at what he had done.

Soon a sound of thunder was heard among the rocks, and Loki knew that Thor was near at hand. He did not feel altogether comfortable as he heard the god draw near, for he had felt his power more than once, and he began to think it might not be altogether pleasant to meet him in the first burst of his wrath. So, as Loki could change. himself into any form he pleased, he plunged into the stream and became a salmon-trout, thereby hoping to escape Thor's notice.

But Thor had already seen him, and at the same time his eye fell upon the weeping Sif, shorn of all her hair.

'Who has done this?' he asked.

'Loki,' sobbed Sif.

'Thou caitiff,' said Thor, addressing himself to the salmon-trout, 'thou shalt be sorely punished for what thou hast done.' And changing himself into a huge sea-gull Thor dived into the water and seized the salmon-trout in his beak.

'Now will I break all thy bones, as a miller crushes the grain to powder,' exclaimed Thor.

Then Loki took again his own shape and answered:

'If you break my bones to pieces and scatter them to the winds, it will not help to bring back Sif's hair. Now, if you will only spare me this time I will get fairer tresses for Sif than those she has lost. This I swear by the eye of Odin, by the moss on the grave of the wise Mimir, and, greater than all, by thy wondrous hammer.'

Then Thor thundered forth, 'Thou knave, how darest thou swear by my hammer? Dost thou not know that Miölnir is hidden beneath the waters ? '

Then Loki shook and trembled like an aspen leaf, but he found voice to answer, 'If thou wilt spare me this once, O mighty Thor, I will go to my kinsmen, the dwarfs, and from them I can get whatever I ask for. In their underground kingdom there are wonderful forges, and they can make for thee a better hammer than the one thou hast lost. Spare me this once, O most gracious Thor, spare me !'

' No,' said Thor, 'I will not spare thee. Thou dost deserve death, and death shall be thy fate. I have come hither with Freyr, my sworn comrade, and we will have thy life.'

Then Loki fell weeping at the feet of Freyr. ' O Freyr, have pity upon me. Prevail upon Thor to forgive me, and I will bring thee a courser the like of which hath never been seen. Never shall he grow weary, though thou shouldst ride him day and night. He shall gallop alike over land and sea, and from his hair shall come a bright light that will light thee on the darkest midnight.'

And Loki begged so earnestly and swore so solemnly and promised repentance so fairly, that

at length Thor and Freyr let him go on condition
that he should bring them the gifts he promised.

So Loki slunk away, and down he crept through
the cold hard rocks into the colder earth, down,
down, until he came to the underground world
where the dwarfs were at work.

Loki was not sorry to feel the pleasant warmth
of the forge fires, for he had had a very chilling
journey, and the bright ruddy glow of the flames
was a cheerful sight, and there was something lifelike
and cheering in the sharp ring of the hammers,
and in the roaring of the great bellows. It was
wonderful to see the dwarfs in their leather aprons
working away so busily and hammering the brown
stone into pure gold.

But if this were wonderful, it was equally
wonderful and perhaps a more beautiful sight to
see them make precious stones out of common
rock-crystal. Some they tinged with dye got
from deep crimson rosebuds, and lo they made
rubies and carbuncles. Into some they pressed
the juice of early violets, and behold there glittered
priceless sapphires ; whilst the purple grape juice
and the greenest grasses furnished delicate tints
for amethysts and emeralds.

SIF'S GOLDEN HAIR.

'It was wonderful to see the dwarfs in their leather aprons working away so busily' (p. 78).

It was a wonderful place, this underground world of the dwarfs, and they kept their secrets carefully from the people of the upper world.

'Welcome,' said Dvalin, one of the dwarfs, to Loki; 'welcome to our kingdom. What errand may have brought you hither?'

Then Loki told how he had charmed away Sif's hair, and that he wanted new ringlets for her, and a steed for Freyr, a new hammer for Thor, and a ring for Odin.

'All these shalt thou have, and of the best,' returned Dvalin; 'thou art our kinsman, and it shall never be said that the dwarfs failed in their friendship.'

Then the dwarfs took the skin of a wild boar and threw it into the furnace, where the flames leaped round it till it turned red and seemed to be consumed by a million tiny stars, then it burned and burned until we might think that it must have been burnt to tinder; but it was not so. It had simply grown into a solid block at which the dwarfs pounded away with their sledge-hammers as if it had been a piece of red-hot iron.

Then again they thrust it into the furnace, and taking their bellows blew the flames into such a roaring sparkling column that Loki half thought they meant to set the upper-world on fire, and whilst some blew the others plied their hammers so quickly that the cave rang with the clang of their blows.

Now all this time Loki was sitting by, regretting that he had made so many promises and sorry to see how well the work was going on. For now that he was safely away from Thor and Freyr he did not wish them to have the wonderful gifts that he had promised to get for them, and though he knew that he should be obliged to keep his word, he determined that if he could in any way injure his kinsmen's work he would do so.   So he changed himself into a venomous fly and perched upon the wrist of Brokur who was blowing the bellows· Happily Brokur's skin was so tough that he did not feel the bite that Loki gave him and went on blowing steadily, and in due time the work was finished and out of the fire leaped the golden-haired Gullinbörst, the most wonderful wild-boar that was ever heard of, and this was the fleet steed that Freyr the sun-god was to have to carry him round the world.

Then the dwarfs set to work to make the ring

for Odin, and a wonderful ring it was, of broad gold, shaped like a serpent with its tail in its mouth, and studded all over with precious stones. This was the ring Dröpner that afterwards became so well known.

No sooner was it finished than the unwearied dwarfs set to work again to make the hammer for Thor ; and for this purpose they took a bar of cold iron, which, without heating, they began to beat with their hammers.

They used neither file nor fire ; yet it grew shapely and strong beneath their even blows. Loki soon saw that this hammer would be better than Miölnir, and vexed exceedingly, he determined to do his best that it might not be as perfect as the dwarfs wished to make it.

After some thought as to the best means of doing his work, he changed himself into a hornet and stung the chief worker so terribly on the forehead that the blood gushed forth, and the dwarf raising his hand to the wound before the steel was quite beaten out, missed his stroke and so the haft was left an inch too short, and there was not time to make another. Still, in spite of this, the

G

hammer was a very strong hammer, much stronger than Loki wished it to be.

All the gifts were now ready excepting the hair for Sif. But this was not the work of Dvalin or Brokur.

At the other end of the cave sat a dwarf woman with a spinning-wheel, and presently an elf bearing a load of gold upon his head came to her. The dwarf woman took the gold and began to spin it into a slender thread, and as she spun she sang this song:

> 'Golden hair I spin
> For Sif the fair—
> Golden hair I spin
> Bright beyond compare.
> Golden hair I spin,
> It shall bring her love—
> Golden hair I spin,
> Not e'en the queen above
> Can such beauteous tresses show
> As these that o'er Sif's neck shall flow.
> Golden hair I spin, I spin,
> Nought shall harm these locks of gold,
> Magic spell, nor malice bold;
> Golden locks I spin, I spin.'

And then the dwarf-woman rolled the golden thread into a great ball, and after snipping it in several places with her long scissors shook it out, and it fell into the most lovely ringlets possible.

She gave the glossy tresses to Loki, who was very sorry to see how beautiful they were.

'As soon as they touch Sif's head,' said the dwarf woman, 'they will grow to it just like her own hair.'

'Will they?' said Loki rather curtly, for he was not half so well pleased with the dwarf woman's success as she was herself.

'And Sif will be more beautiful than ever!' she added.

But Loki moved away so as not to hear what she was saying; and, bidding the dwarfs farewell, he departed with his presents to the upper regions.

Thor was delighted with the hair and confessed that Loki had indeed kept his promise well. The hammer too was far beyond his hopes, and he was quite satisfied with it.

Freyr too was overjoyed at the sight of Gullenbörst, and, leaping on its back, rode away at full speed.

As for Sif, she danced for joy when Thor brought her the golden locks, and her fingers trembled so that she could scarcely put them on. However, the curls seemed to go right of themselves; and as the old dwarf woman had said, they grew to her head at once, and were even more shining and beautiful than her own hair had been.

The ring was brought to Odin on a great feast-day, and it was agreed that all Loki's previous misdoings should be pardoned because he had kept his promises so well.

So Loki was forgiven ; but as he was always happiest when he was in mischief it is not to be supposed that he would remain very long without again offending the gods.

VI.

THE WONDERFUL QUERN STONES.

ONCE upon a time there was a king of Denmark
or Gotland, as it was then called, whose name was
Frothi. He was a great-grandson of the god Thor
and a very mighty king, and wherever the Danish
language was spoken there was Frothi's name
honoured and respected.

Among his treasures were two quern stones;
nothing much to look at, simply two common mill
stones in appearance, and no one who did not
know what they could do would think of taking
any notice of them. Nevertheless, these quern
stones were of more worth than anything that
King Frothi had, for they could produce anything
that the grinder of the quern or handmill wished
for. They would bring gold, silver, precious stones,
anything and everything; and besides this they
could grind love, joy, peace; therefore it is not too
much to say that these stones were worth more
than all the treasures of the king put together.

At least they would have been if he could have
made use of them, but they were so heavy that
few could be found to turn the quern, and just at
the time of which I am speaking there was no one
at all in the land of Gotland able to work away at
the quern handle.

Now the more King Frothi pondered over his
wonderful quern stones, the greater became his
desire to use them, and he sought throughout the
land from north to south, from east to west, if perchance he might find some one strong enough to
help him in his need. But all to no purpose,
and he was utterly in despair when, by good
luck, he happened to go on a visit to Fiölnir,
king of Sweden, and to hear of two slave-women
of great size and strength. Surely, thought Frothi,
these are just the women to grind at my quern
Grotti (for so it was called), and he asked King
Fiölnir to be allowed to see them.

So King Fiölnir ordered the slaves to be brought
before Frothi, and when Frothi saw them his spirits
rose, for certainly Menia and Fenia were strong-
looking women. They were eight feet in height,
and broader across the shoulders than any of
Frothi's warriors, and the muscles of their arms

stood out like cords. And they lifted heavy weights, threw heavy javelins, and did so many feats of strength that Frothi felt quite sure that they would be able to turn the quern handle.

'I will buy these slaves,' said he, 'and take them with me to Gotland.'

Menia and Fenia stood with their arms folded and their proud heads bowed down, whilst Frothi counted out the gold to the seller. They were slaves; with money had they been bought, with money were they sold again. What cared Frothi who was their father, or how they had come into the land of Sweden?

And he took them home with him and bade them grind at the quern. Now he should be able to test the power of the wonderful stones.

'Grind, grind, Menia and Fenia, let me see whether ye have strength for the work.'

So spake King Frothi, and the huge women lifted the heavy stones as though they had been pebbles.

'What shall we grind?' asked the slaves.

'Gold, gold, peace and wealth for Frothi.'

Gold! gold! the land was filled with riches. Treasure in the king's palace, treasure in the

coffers of his subjects—gold! gold! There were
no poor in the land, no beggars in the streets, no
children crying for bread. All honour to the quern
stones !

Peace ! peace ! no more war in the land, Frothi
is at peace with everyone. And more than that,
there was peace in all countries where Frothi's
name was known, even to the far south ; and
everyone talked of Frothi's peace. Praise be to
the quern stones !

Wealth ! yes, everything went well. Not one
of the counsels of King Frothi failed. There was
not a green field that did not yield a rich crop;
not a tree but bent beneath its weight of fruit ; not
a stream that ran dry; not a vessel that sailed
from the harbours of Gotland that came not back,
after a fair voyage, in safety to its haven. There
was good luck everywhere.

'Grind on, grind on, Menia and Fenia! good fortune is mine,' said King Frothi.

And the slaves ground on.

'When shall we rest, when may we rest, King
Frothi ? It is weary work toiling day and night.'

'No longer than whilst the cuckoo is silent in
the spring.'

'Never ceasing is the cry of the cuckoo in the groves ; may we not rest longer?'

'Not longer,' answered King Frothi, 'than whilst the verse of a song is sung.'

'That is but little!' sighed Menia and Fenia, and they toiled on. Their arms were weary and their eyes heavy, they would fain have slept; but Frothi would not let them have any sleep. They were but slaves who must obey their master, so they toiled on, still grinding peace and wealth to Frothi—

> 'To Frothi and his queen
>   Joy and peace—
> May plenty in the land
>   Still increase,
> Frothi and his queen
>   From dangers keep ;
> May they on beds of down
>   Sweetly sleep.
> No sword be drawn
>   In Gotland old,
> By murderer bold.
>   No harm befall
> The high or low—
>   To none be woe,
> Good luck to all.
>   Good luck to all,
> We grind, we grind.
>   No rest we find,
>   For rest we call.'

Thus sang the two giant women; then they begged again, 'Give us rest, O Frothi!'

But still Frothi answered, 'Rest whilst the verse of a song is sung, or as long as the cuckoo is silent in the spring.'

No longer would the king give them.

Yet Frothi was deemed a good king, but gold and good luck were hardening his heart.

Menia and Fenia went on grinding and their wrath grew deeper and deeper, and thus at last they spoke.

First said Fenia, 'Thou wert not wise, O Frothi. Thou didst buy us because like giants we towered above the other slaves, because we were strong and hardy and could lift heavy burdens.'

And Menia took up the wail: 'Are we not of the race of the mountain giants? Are not our kindred greater than thine, O Frothi? The quern had never left the grey fell but for the giants' daughters. Never, never should we have ground as we have done, had it not been that we remembered from what race we sprang.'

Then answered Menia: 'Nine long winters saw us training to feats of strength, nine long winters of wearisome labour. Deep down in the earth we toiled and toiled until we could move the high mountain from its foundations. We are weird women, O Frothi. We can see far into the future. Our eyes have looked upon the quern before. In the giants' house we whirled it until the earth shook, and hoarse thunder resounded through the caverns. Thou art not wise, O Frothi. O Frothi, thou art not wise!'

But Frothi heard them not; he was sleeping the sweet sleep that the quern stones had ground for him.

'Strong are we indeed,' laughed Fenia, sorrow-fully, 'strong to contend with the puny men. We, whose pastime in Sweden was to tame the fiercest bears, so that they ate from our hands. We who fought with mighty warriors and came off con-querors. We who helped one prince and put down another. Well we fought, and many were the wounds we received from sharp spears and flashing swords. Frothi knows not our power, or he would scarce have brought us to his palace to treat us thus. Here no one has compassion upon us. Cold are the skies above us, and the pitiless wind beats upon our breast. Cold is the ground on which we stand, and the keen frost bites our feet. Ah, there are none to pity us. No one cares for the slaves. We grind for ever an enemy's quern, and he gives us no rest. Grind, grind; I am weary of grinding; I must have rest.'

'Nay,' returned Menia, 'talk not of rest until Frothi is content with what we bring him.'

Then Fenia started: 'If he gives us no rest, let us take it ourselves. Why should we any longer grind good for him who only gives us evil? We can grind what we please. Let us revenge our-selves.'

Then Menia turned the handle quicker than ever, and in a wild voice she sang:

> 'I see a ship come sailing
> With warriors bold aboard,
> There's many a one that in Danish blood
> Would be glad to dip his sword.
> Say shall we grind them hither?
> Say shall they land to-night?
> Say shall they set the palace a-fire?
> Say shall they win the fight?'

Then called Fenia in a voice of thunder through the midnight air: 'Frothi, Frothi, awake, awake! Wilt thou not listen to us? Have mercy and let us rest our weary limbs.'

THE WONDERFUL QUERN-STONES.

'Again Fenia shouted "Frothi Frothi, awake! the beacon is blazing"' (p. 93).

But all was still, and Frothi gave no answer to the cry.

'Nay,' answered Menia, 'he will not hearken. Little he cares for the worn-out slaves. Revenge, revenge!'

And Frothi slept, not dreaming of the evil that was coming upon him.

And again Fenia shouted: 'Frothi, Frothi, awake! The beacon is blazing. Danger is nigh. Wilt thou not spare?'

But Frothi gave no answer, and the giant women toiled on.

'O Frothi, Frothi, we cannot bear our weariness.'

And still no answer came.

'Frothi, Frothi, danger is nigh thee. Well-manned ships are gliding over the sea. It is Mysingr who comes, his white sail flutters in the wind. His flag is unfurled. Frothi, Frothi, awake, awake! thou shalt be king no longer.'

And as the giant women ground, the words they spake came to pass, they were grinding revenge for themselves, and brought the enemy nearer and nearer.

'Ho! hearkne to the herald! Frothi, Frothi, the

town is on fire. The palaces will soon be ruined
heaps. Grind, Menia, ever more swiftly, until we
grind death to Frothi.'

And Menia and Fenia ground and ground till
Mysingr and his followers landed from the ships.
They ground until they had reached the palace.

'To arms, to arms,' shouted the warders, but it
was too late. The Gotlanders armed themselves;
but who could stand against the army that the
slave women were grinding against them?

Not long did the struggle last. Frothi and his
Gotlanders fought bravely, but the sea-king and
his allies were mightier, for the giantesses were in
giant mood, and turned the handle faster and
faster, until down fell the quern stones. Then
sank Frothi pierced with wounds, and the fight
was over. The army that Menia and Fenia had
ground to help Mysingr vanished; and Mysingr
and his men alone were left conquerors on the
bloody field.

They loaded their ships with treasure, and
Mysingr took with him Menia, Fenia, and the
quern stones.

But, alas! Mysingr was no wiser than King
Frothi had been.

Gold, however, was not his first thought; he had enough of that, but he wanted something else that just then was more to him than gold.

There was no salt on board the sea-king's vessels; so he said, 'Grind salt.'

And Menia and Fenia ground salt for Mysingr.

At midnight they asked if they had ground enough.

And Mysingr bade them grind on.

And so they ground and ground until the ship was so heavy with salt that it sank, and the sea-king and all his men were drowned.

Where the quern stones went down there is to this day a great whirlpool, and the waters of the sea have been salt ever since.

VII.

THORWALD'S BRIDAL.

DESOLATE is the cold dark north, with its ice-walls and its ice-citadels rising amidst everlasting snows.

Well does the north king guard his fortress, so that few dare approach it, for he breathes death on those who rashly seek to do battle with him, and bleached bones show to them the fate of those who have gone before.

The Elivâgi issuing from dreary Niflheim have thrown up their waters in rimy spray, which has frozen into fantastic shapes, and Ginnungagap, grown wider and wider, sends forth a death-blast to mortal men.

Dreary is the north, what beauty is to be seen in it? The tall pine trees with their thick bristling crowns wave solemnly and shadow the deep lakes and the steep hill-sides, but even they draw not nigh to the ice-palace where the grey old monarch, with frosty beard and crown of icicles, sits on his

awful throne. Like a statue, he sits with his white -
robed menials, who stand spell-bound like mournful ghosts, nor stir till, at the raising of his sceptre,
they flee forth to plant the north king's banner in
sunnier lands.

Southward, southward, to catch a glimpse of
beauty and to die—for the sun-god fights for the
fairer lands, and the ice-clad army with their hail-
slings and their frosted spears, fades away as his
great flaming sword leaps from its scabbard. So
they perish, but they have seen before they die the
soul-entrancing beauty which they dreamed of in
their dreams.

Yet there is beauty in the rugged north, when
Night drives through the dark blue vault with her
black courser, and the golden stars shine out as
lamps along her heavenly path. Around her flash,
in bars of brilliant radiance, fair lights that, stream-
ing athwart the northern skies, light up the masses
of ice which the Elivâgi roll up from Niflheim.

And there is beauty in the north when the beautiful Day wakes up from peaceful slumbers in his
mother's arms, and gaily springs into his glittering
chariot. Lightly he seizes the reins, and at his
touch, Skinfaxi paws the air and shakes his glowing

H

mane, and sparks of dazzling light float around, and
the heavens are lit up with their splendour. The
stars hide their heads, and the moon turns pale, and
the ice-rocks glitter in a brighter and fresher light.

And if for a moment the lovely bridge should
be seen that stretches its gem-studded archway
from earth to heaven, the blue and rose-stained
crystal peaks quiver with rays of amethyst and
emerald.

No mortal hath yet found the spot on earth
whence the arch springs, else would he find a
treasure hidden by the gods of old, that would
make him rich beyond his fellows, and wiser too,
for when the foundations of the bridge were laid,
Odin, the All Father, whispered words of deep wisdom into the earth, that have lain buried there for
long ages.

And when this corner stone of Bifröst is found,
those words shall issue forth like sweet-toned music,
and fill the soul of the finder with the wisdom of
the gods; and in his heart shall rise such undreamed-
of sense of bliss, that he will never care to leave
the earth.

So ran the old tale, and Thorwald believed in it,
and many an hour and many a day he spent in

searching for the stone that would bring not only wealth, but happiness and wisdom, and open to him the pathway of the gods. For Thorwald's heart told him that there were higher things than those on earth. A voice was ever crying, 'seek, seek,' and his heart-strings vibrated to the sound.

He sought amidst Norwegian Fjelds, for there have the Jötuns left their traces, and he thought that perchance amongst the huge boulders the Asi might have laid the corner-stone of Bifröst.

Often did he wander for days without catching a glimpse of its brilliant colours ; then all at once some distant spot would be bathed in its rays, and he would dart forward, hoping to find, amidst blue and crimson flowers, that which he sought. But as he drew near, the blue and crimson blossoms had paled into the purest white, and the rainbow was dying away behind the clouds.

Then would wild bursts of unearthly laughter issue from the pine-grove, but no one was in sight. Louder and shriller the laughter resounded, and Thorwald knew that it was the Skogsra or wood-spirit, and he must take heed how he answered it.

Yet he was undaunted, and each fresh disappointment seemed but to give him more strength,

and still his song breathed, 'Hope! hope!'
The world was wide before him, life was in its
spring-tide, the sun was riding high in the glorious
noon, and time spread out a never-ending stream
that glided at his feet.   And as he went his way,
the forest rang with echoes of his sweet spirit-stir-
ring voice.   The branches waved as if to cheer him
on his way, and the birds answered the burden of
his song, and soared aloft as though luring him to
follow them into the calm blue heights above.

And Thorwald's soul fled after them, and rose
higher and higher than their flight.   Soon would
he have gained the realms of the gods, and the fair
halls of Gimli be open to him.

'Hope, hope,' he sang, 'art thou the bridge that
bears man up to heaven?'

Onward and ever onward he travelled, and turning his back on the cold north, he wended southward like the north king's army, trusting to find in
more genial lands the treasure which he sought.

Suddenly, a jagged bough shot out before him,
that seemed with straggling fingers to point the
way which he should take.   So at least Thorwald
thought, and he went musing on.

He had not gone far, before he heard a low song

that came stealing through the trees like the whisper of the softest summer breeze, so sweet, so low, that he paused, fearful lest his foot-fall might disturb it. And as he listened, the sad notes filled his heart with pity, and a gentle sadness stole over him.

He gave a sigh; but the voice did not cease, and Thorwald stole breathlessly towards the singer, and forgot the bridge Bifröst in the spell that was cast over him. He could now hear the words distinctly,

'No hope, no hope,
Lost, lost, for evermore ;
Barred is the golden door,
Closed is the golden gate.
Lost, lost—too late, too late !
There is no path to heaven
For us to tread ;
There is no quiet grave,
No silent bed
Wherein to lie at rest, for rest hath fled ;
Lost, lost—too late, too late ! '

And as the last words died away, they were followed by deep sobs, and Thorwald, going nearer, saw a fair maiden with her arms clasped round the trunk of a moss-grown pine, weeping bitterly.

Thorwald was greatly moved at her grief, and as he gazed upon her, the bow shone out and its glorious rays fell upon the figure of the kneeling maiden.

' Bifröst, Bifröst ! ' murmured Thorwald, ' thou art found,' and he sprang forward to mark the spot ; but when he reached it there was no trace of the rainbow left, and he clasped the weeping damsel in his arms.

She rose, and looked in wonderment on Thorwald. The rainbow had left its violet light in her eyes, and its ruby dye yet flushed her cheek and lips. Her waving hair fell like a veil around her, as with crossed arms she stood mute before him.

Then there sprang up in Thorwald's heart a feeling he had never known before, sweeter than all the dreams of his soul ; and he thought that perchance he had found the secret of all wisdom that Odin had whispered into the earth — the precious stone from which upstarted the pathway to heaven.

It seemed to him as though a fountain of joy had burst forth and was overflowing the world, whilst above him floated clouds of incense whose edges were gilded with the rays of a newly risen-sun, and the sun's name was Love.

He turned to the maiden : ' And art thou also seeking the road to heaven ? ' he asked.

Then the maiden's tears fell fast, and she answered : ' The gate is closed upon us, we cannot enter.'

' Nay,' replied Thorwald, ' wilt thou not let me lead thee thither ? I have found the corner-stone, and we will tread the pathway of the gods together.'

Then she arose, and casting her silver harp into the stream, she said : ' Go, bear the tidings of my happiness to my kindred. Never again shall my touch awake thy mournful strains. A golden-stringed harp shall be mine, and wood and hill shall echo to my song of rejoicing.'

And Huldra took Thorwald's hand and kissed it. Now should she become one of the mortal race.

' We will go home,' said Thorwald.

And the words sank into the maiden's heart, filling it with deep peace. . . . .

. . . . . .

' I have found the gate of heaven,' said Thorwald to his mother; ' Love can carry the human soul high above the world, until it finds a dwelling-place in Gladsheim, a home among the gods.'

The mother smiled sadly, for she had had her dream in youth, but it had vanished, and she had not yet reached heaven. Nevertheless, she answered gently, ' Be it so, my son,' for she hoped a better lot might be his, and she loved Huldra for Thorwald's sake, and entered into his dreams.

The wedding feast was made ready and the guests were bidden, and Huldra prayed that she might send for some of her own people to be present at her marriage.

'They are not far off,' she said, 'the harp bore a message to them.' And so the shapely Trolls mingled with the wedding guests, but none knew them from human beings save Thorwald and Huldra. And they ate of the feast and joined in the dance, and drank health and happiness to the bride and bridegroom. And Thorwald's cup of joy was overflowing, and he stepped aside from the gay throng to dwell for a moment in silent thankfulness upon his happiness.

He threw himself upon the mossy turf, smooth as velvet, and looking up into the skies, he saw the shadowy bridge far, far away, floating in mid air; and as he cast down his dazzled eyes, lo! the bright-coloured beams played on a mound of earth close to the spot whereon he rested.

Perchance it was the treasure-mound wherein lay the coffer hidden by the gods, the golden treasure!

' O Thorwald ! hast thou not enough already ? '

Not for himself; he wished no greater treasure for himself than that which he already had, but who knew what rare-fashioned jewels might be buried there which would gladden the eyes of Huldra ?

And he thrust his sword deep into the mound.

It struck against something hard, and Thorwald staggered back as though he had received a blow, but before he had time to recover from it, he found himself seated at a festive board, around which tiny elves were holding uproarious revelry. And one advancing with a goblet, begged Thorwald to drink to the health of the Elfin-king and queen before he went back to his own bridal feast. So Thorwald drained the cup, and would have returned it to the hand of the elf who brought it; but the elfin train had vanished, and he found himself stretched on the mossy turf.

The mound had disappeared, and he turned his face in wonder towards the place where he had left his bride. But everything seemed strange to him : there were no signs of feasting ; no wedding guests ; no bride ; but all was silent. The old grey tower that he called home was an ivy-grown ruin ; people whose faces he knew not were

wandering hither and thither, and seemed surprised to see a knight in rich costume roaming
through the woods and fields.

Thorwald was as one stunned.   What had
happened ?   He had left his home but a moment
since.   How, then, should it be thus changed ?

He stopped an aged peasant woman.   'Where
are the bridal guests that feasted here but a moment
ago ?' he asked.

But the old crone made no answer, she only
stared at him in amazement.

'I am the bridegroom, where is my bride, where
is Huldra ?'

Then the old crone started, for she thought of
a strange story of a wedding that had taken place
in her grandmother's days, and that she had often
heard of when a little child.

'There has been no bride called Huldra in these
parts,' she said, 'since Thorwald the bard vanished at
his marriage feast ; but that is a hundred years ago.'

A hundred years !   And the heart of Thorwald
sank within him.

'Tell me the story.'

Then the crone began : 'More than a hundred
years ago, there lived a strange poet who dreamed

that he might find the path that led from earth to heaven. He journeyed forth——'

But here Thorwald stopped her: 'Nay, nay, good mother,' quoth he, 'I know all that, tell me of the wedding feast, the bride——'

And the old woman went on: 'The wedding guests were bidden to the feast——'

But again Thorwald hurriedly broke in on her words.

'Tell me how the bridegroom vanished,' he asked.

'The bridegroom was missed from the feast; far and near, high and low, they sought him, but he could nowhere be found. Some said that he was carried away by the Trolls; others that he had found the spot where Bifröst touches the earth, and that he had crossed it and gained the regions of the gods, and that there in the halls of Gimli he had forgotten his bride. But how it was none ever knew. The bride was wild with grief, and sought after Thorwald twenty days and nights and never rested, and when she came to the place where two streams meet, and where, as the story goes, she had thrown her silver harp away when she first met with Thorwald, she sank down under a stately pine tree.

There she died; and there she is buried. Her last
words were: 'Hope! hope! O Thorwald! thou
hast given me heaven.'

Thorwald's heart stood still, his dream of bliss
was shattered, and the world grew dark. The
treasure, if indeed he had found it, had been
snatched away, to show him that on earth is no
undying happiness. His high hopes died away, he
turned from the wondering crone, and sought the
grave of Huldra. And there, in his bitter grief, he
wept and called aloud: 'O Huldra! Huldra!'

And through the pine-grove came an echo back,
clear and sweet, unlike an earthly voice, and it
answered: 'Huldra! Huldra!'

It sounded so far off that Thorwald thought that
a voice had spoken to him from heaven.

And as he gazed upward Bifröst once more
shone out, brighter and more beautiful than ever.
Thorwald could see clearly now its golden arches
dipping into a sea of blue, and its stones of brilliant
hues flashing in the sunlight. It rested at his feet,
then far away it stretched till it was lost in heaven,
and where it touched the clouds he saw the form of
his beloved Huldra. A sparkling crown was on
her brow, she smiled lovingly and stretched out

her arms towards him. And as she smiled, he heard a solemn whisper issue from the ground: 'Through death alone can mortals gain the joy that shall know no end.'

Perhaps this was the secret that Odin had buried long since in the earth.

;   .   .   .   .   .

The body of Thorwald was never found. The peasants believe that unseen hands laid him in the grave beside Huldra, and that the course of the river was changed so that their resting-place might never be known.

Yet if some poet-dreamer should find the spot where the bright rainbow takes root in the earth, he may rest assured that he has found the grave of Thorwald and his bride.

VIII.

CHRISTIN'S TROUBLE.

THERE was once a very beautiful maiden whose name was Christin, and she was betrothed to a noble knight.

Christin had long yellow locks, and when the sun shone upon them they glittered so brightly that one might almost believe they were threads of gold. But when Sir Peter stroked little Christin's shining hair he knew that no gold was ever half so soft.

Sir Peter was a very valiant knight and little Christin loved him with all her heart, and as he also loved her, it would seem that there was no cause for her to be unhappy. Nevertheless she was unhappy, and she wept so sorely that Sir Peter was much grieved, and tried to find out what was the reason of her tears.

'My heart's dear,' said Sir Peter, 'tell me what hath vexed thee.'

But Christin's sobs prevented her from replying;

she tried to speak, but the words died away upon her lips.

Now it happened that Sir Peter had been amusing himself in the courtyard, and he thought that this might in some way have annoyed the maiden.

'Is it saddle or steed that does not please thee?' he asked.

But that was not the trouble.

'Dost thou not love me?' said the Knight. 'Canst thou be grieving that thou art to be my bride?'

'Nay, nay,' replied Christin at last, 'it is not that I grieve for.'

'Wherefore then dost thou weep, since to-day is to be thy wedding day?'

'Ah!' answered Christin, 'it is because I fear lest what was said when I was a child should come true to-day. It was ever told me that some great evil should happen to me on my wedding day; and now I tremble as I think of passing over the waters of Ringfalla. Two of my sisters were lost in its deceitful depths, and I am afraid of a like fate for myself. Alas, alas! these yellow locks that you prize so much may be wet beneath the cold

waves of Ringfalla ere the sun goes down. I see
my lost sisters ever before me, and they beckon to
me to join them deep down below the flood.'

Then Sir Peter tried to comfort Christin, and he
bade her take courage, for everything should be
done to prevent any harm from happening to her.
And, as the greatest safeguard he could think of,
he promised that the horse she rode should be
shod with golden shoes nailed on with golden nails,
so that it would be impossible for it to stumble or
meet with any mishap.

'And besides that,' he added, 'you shall be well
guarded, little Christin, for twelve of my courtiers
shall ride before you, and twelve at either side, so
that you need have no cause for fear.'

Still Christin wept bitterly. Perhaps she had
not so much faith in golden shoes as other people
had. But if she did not trust much in the shoes,
perhaps she had some confidence when she saw
the brave train of courtiers who were to attend her.
Surely they would guard her in case of danger,
and even if she fell into the waters of Ringfalla,
there were arms strong enough to save her.

A gallant train they were, in their silks and
velvets and holiday plumes, and their scabbards

gleamed with costly gems, and gay were the trap-
pings of the milk-white palfrey that Christin was
to ride. The saddle-cloth was of purple fringed
with gold, and as the palfrey pawed the ground its
golden shoes flashed like fire.

Christin began to forget her troubles at the
sight of the splendour before her. She dried her
tears, and the wedding train went merrily onward.

They rode and rode until the forest of Ringfalla
came in sight, and the green boughs waved as
though they would welcome the bride.

They rode on and on until they reached the
forest and found themselves in its pleasant shade.
Wide spread the branched ceiling above them, and
the birds twittered a song of greeting. The sun
peeped through the leafy archways, and sent slant-
ing rays of light that flickered on the pathway and
rested on the edges of the fragrant blossoms. It
was very beautiful, so beautiful that Christin's
sorrow was quite hushed, and she gazed in delight
through the tall ferns, and tangled bushes, and
slender tree stems until they became indistinct in
the distance; or she turned her eyes upward
through the twining tracery of the branches, and

I

caught a glimpse of the summer sky that seemed like an arch of sapphire.

Meanwhile the courtiers were attracted by a very different sight, and truly it was something marvellous that they beheld.

A deer with golden horns. Such a deer had never been seen before, so slender, so graceful, with eyes that shone like diamonds, and above all, with golden horns. No wonder they should look upon it as a prize. A stag's head with golden horns would be a trophy worth having. It was too great a temptation for the courtiers to resist.

So the twelve courtiers in front, and the twelve on either side, and we are not told how many more, fell to hunting the wonderful deer.

And poor little Christin was left almost alone, there was no one with her but Sir Peter. The waters of Ringfalla were close at hand, and in another minute she would have to pass over the bridge she so much dreaded with nothing to trust to but her horse's golden shoes.

Doubtless she felt very much frightened, but there was no help for it, she must cross the bridge on the way to the church.

Go on, good steed ; may thy golden shoes enable thee to carry little Christin over in safety !

Alas ! alas ! In spite of the golden shoes, the palfrey stumbled, and little Christin was thrown into the calm, still waters.

Down, down she sank, deep down ; and before Sir Peter had even time to dismount she was no longer to be seen.

He would have plunged in to save her ; but this he knew would be of no avail, and they would both perish in Ringfalla's flood.

He turned, therefore, to his little footpage.

'Go swiftly,' quoth he, 'and bring me my golden harp.'

And the footpage mounted his master's charger and away he rode full fleetly.

It seemed an age to Sir Peter till the page returned, but he came at last bearing the harp with him.

Now it may be asked, of what use can a harp be to drowning people ?

It would be none at all now-a-days, but then these are not the days of wonders. Those old fairy times have passed away, and there is no trace of them left upon the earth.

Then, too, it may be said: 'Surely Christin must be dead by this time, she has been so long under the water.'

Ah! but she has not been drowning; she has been visiting a mighty palace underneath the waves of Ringfalla, and has seen sights of which mortals have never dreamed,—strange water-plants whose flowers have petals of pure crystal, and whose long leaves are like bands of soft green velvet, twisting round the pillars of the palace. And great shining pebbles of blue, and green, and crimson studding the yellow sand. And curious creatures of brilliant hues, of every shape and size, crawling, or swimming, or darting hither and thither on delicate wing-like fins, so that one might suppose them to be water-butterflies.

And Christin knows that in this river-palace she must live for ever if Sir Peter should not be able to win her back from the ugly sprite who has made her his captive as he did her two sisters long ago.

And whilst she is thinking of all this, and the ugly sprite is sitting grinning at her, suddenly a sound so soft and beautiful comes through the

CHRISTIN'S TROUBLE.

'As the ugly sprite heard it he sprang ashore' (p. 117).

waters that the ugly sprite leaves off grinning and listens to it attentively.

It is Sir Peter striking the first chord on his harp.

And the ugly sprite, turning away from Christin, rose up to the top of the flood, and there he sat upon a wave and laughed.

Sir Peter spoke no word, but he struck the harp a second time.

And a sweet murmuring note stole over the waters, and the waves carried it on and on until it died away for ever.

And as the ugly sprite heard it he sprang ashore, and, throwing himself on the mossy turf, he wept aloud.

Still Sir Peter spoke never a word, but struck his harp for the third time.

And a soft white arm was raised above the stream. It was little Christin's arm.

But Sir Peter spake never a word, but still went on playing.

Presently Christin lifted her head above the water and looked at him.

Of course Sir Peter was overjoyed, but he did not let his joy run away with his good sense. He knew that what had come to pass was all owing to the golden harp, and he determined, as it had been successful so far, to give it a fair trial.

This was a wise resolve on his part, for, aided by the wonderful music, Christin had grasped some floating lilies which floated her close up to the bank of the river, and she scrambled through the rushes and crept close to Sir Peter.

The beautiful music had saved her!

Now during this time the ugly sprite had been overwhelmed by repentant feelings, and this was what came of it.

He suddenly plunged into the river again, and in another moment Sir Peter and Christin saw him rising to the surface with two fair maidens whom Christin knew at once to be her sisters.

She sprang forward to meet them, but Sir Peter still went on playing, for perchance the ugly sprite might have changed his mind if the music had ceased.

And so Christin and her sisters were brought back from the waters of Ringfalla through the sounds of a golden harp.

The harp was of more use than the golden shoes!

Christin's trouble was over.   The train of

courtiers rejoined Sir Peter again, and they all went merrily on to the church, where Christin and Sir Peter were married.

Doubtless the lost sisters acted as bridesmaids, and afterwards married handsome knights, with whom they lived as happily for ever after as Christin did with Sir Peter.

IX.

HOW THE WOLF FENRIS WAS CHAINED.

In the times when Odin and Thor ruled in Asgard there were giants and monsters of all sorts, and some of the evil gods had monsters for children.

So it was with Loki, who had married Signe, the daughter of one of the Jötuns or giants. Two of his children were Jormungand, the great serpent, and the wolf Fenris ; the third was a daughter named Hela, who, though she was not a monster, was nevertheless very terrible to look upon. They were all born in Jötunheim, where they lived for some time before the Asi heard anything about them.

When at length the tidings that they lived reached the ears of Odin, he felt very uneasy, as did the Asi generally, for they called to mind certain old prophecies, which said that these monsters should arise, and in due time bring great evils both upon gods and men. Nay, it was even said that the wolf Fenris should devour Odin him-

self. Well, therefore, might Odin wish that something should at once be done to curb the growing
power of Loki's offspring. At the same time he
feared to offend Loki, who was his foster-brother.
He had never forgotten the days of their childhood, and would never hold a feast unless Loki
were present.

However, he called together a council of the
Asi, and at length it was agreed that the three
children should be brought from Jötunheim to
some place where they might be more within his
power.

If Odin could have slain them at once, he
would doubtless have been well pleased to do so ;
but this was not in his power. He was only able
to command them, and they were bound to obey
him as the greatest of the gods.

So the summons went forth, and on a given day
Loki, with Hela, Fenris, and Jormungand arrived at
the palace where Odin awaited them, seated upon
his throne, and surrounded by the Asi in their
glittering array.

Loki certainly was not dazzled by the splendour
of the gods, he was used to such displays among
them. Neither did it seem in any way to

move his offspring, who drew near to the steps of
the throne without looking either to the right or
to the left.

Hela was a little in front. Her face was grim
and fierce; half her body was black, half flesh
colour. So terrible was she to look at, that a
shudder ran through the whole assembly as they
gazed upon her awful form.

'It is clear that she belongs not to us,' said one
of the Asi.

And Hela at the words half drew the knife out
of her belt, as though she would strike at the
speaker.

But Odin said, 'Nay, over the Asi thou shalt
have no power. In Midgard, where men dwell,
shalt thou be feared, and thy rule shall be over
those of human race. Sorrowfully shall they own
thee as a sovereign, from whose commands there is
no appeal. Over them shalt thou be queen, and
the greatest of kings shall stand in awe of thee.
Go forth, and from the kingdom I will give thee
send forth thy decrees to the children of men.'

Then Odin gave to Hela a dreary kingdom in
Niflheim, the world of mist that is older than
heaven and earth; and there she had charge

over nine worlds, and had a spacious palace with many halls, but all of them were dark and gloomy.

' The dish that thou shalt eat of shall be hunger,' continued Odin ; 'thy bed shall be the bed of sickness, and its hangings splendid woe. Only the dead shall people thy kingdom, and the light of day shall be shut out from it for ever.'

And Hela, having heard her sentence, turned away with a stony countenance. It mattered little to her where she reigned, so long as she could smite and slay.

Then Jormungand drew near. The slimy monster wound and twisted his huge body towards the throne, and a dull lustre shimmered round his heavy scales. The gods shrank back, for malice flashed from his cruel eyes, and the sound of his hissing was fearful to hear.

But Odin bade him be silent, and the great serpent lowered his head and crouched at the king's feet.

And lo, the palace walls suddenly opened, and over the fair gardens of Asgard came a deep, low murmur, and then a mist appeared in the distance, which, as the Asi gazed, shaped itself into the likeness of a troubled sea. Louder yet grew the murmur until it changed into a deep roar, and the gods all wondered what was coming to pass, for it seemed as though the great ocean that surrounds all lands were rushing onward and would overwhelm the palace.   The waves reared their crests higher and higher, and nearer and nearer rolled the waters.

'It is a miracle!' exclaimed the Asi.

But Odin rose and seized the huge serpent and flung him into the advancing tide.

One heavy plunge, one blinding sheet of mist that hid the sunlight and the bright blue sky, one hideous cry, and then a sudden hush,—and as the white mist cleared away, behold the waters had vanished, and naught was to be seen but the fair land of Asgard.

The ocean had seized its prey, and in its depths the serpent was to grow and grow until at length he should stretch all round the world, and lie there harmless, with his tail in his mouth, until the day of Ragnaröck should dawn.

Then only Fenris was left to receive the sentence of Odin.

The palace walls had closed again, and the king of heaven bid the giant-wolf draw near.

Never had the Asi seen so huge a beast of the kind ; he was, moreover, sleek and well shaped, but his look was full of craft and cunning, and he came stealthily along as though he would beg a milder fate than had befallen his brother Jormungand.

The gods pressed forward to gain a better view of the well formed animal, and praised his shining coat and lithe limbs. What would be his doom? And they waited anxiously to hear what Odin would say.

'What say you to our looking after Fenris ourselves?' asked the king.

Then several of the gods stepped forward, and stroked his sleek sides, and patted his comely head, and the wolf seemed so tame that Odin thought that now at least there was nothing to be feared from him. And in the end it was agreed that Fenris should be brought up among the Asi.

So Fenris was lodged in Asgard; and whilst he was quite young all went on well, though sometimes he showed signs of such fierceness that none but Tyr, who was a son of Odin, and one of the boldest and most stout-hearted among the gods, dared to feed him.

As he grew older his strength increased so greatly that the gods began to fear that in the end he might prove too much for them. They also called to mind the sayings concerning the evil that he was to bring upon them, and they pondered whether they should not bind him fast before he became any stronger.

Now Fenris, although he knew not what the gods were thinking of, began to fear something when he saw that they never came to him singly, but always many together, and were, moreover, well armed, and more than once brought chains with them as if they would use them if they might be able to do so. He resolved, therefore, to keep watch.

'If they want to bind me,' said he to himself, 'they must find stronger chains than any that have been forged in Asgard.' Still he pretended not to see what they were doing.

'I wonder if you are as strong as I am,' said Thor to the wolf. 'See, I can break this chain asunder easily. If you were bound with it, could you do the same?'

'Try me,' answered Fenris, who saw at a glance that the chain was not too strong for him. And he allowed it to be wound round and round his body, and fastened to a great iron staple that ran many feet into the earth. Then he shook himself three times, and the third time the fetters fell to the ground, and he was free.

'I can break a stronger chain than that,' said Fenris.

And the gods went away, and made another chain heavier and thicker than the last, and called it Dromi.

Then again they came to Fenris, and asked him if he were willing to try his strength once more.

Fenris eyed the chain narrowly, but feeling that he had strength enough to break it suffered himself again to be bound, and, as before, he broke the chain in pieces, and the splinters flew far and near. And the gods were filled with dismay, for Fenris was already beyond their power to bind. What were they to do?

Bragi, the eloquent god, stepped forward, and in a long speech, in which he taught them that iron and base metal could not overcome such strength as that of Fenris, he told them that from more subtle elements a magic cord might be woven that would resist the wolf's most vigorous efforts.

'But where may we get such a cord?' asked Tyr.

'We have forged to the best of our power, and are unable to make a chain that can hold the monster.'

'The gods are not blacksmiths,' returned Bragi; 'send to those who are. The dwarfs of Black-Elf-land understand the secrets of the craft better than we do.'

Now the region of Black-Elfland, where the dwarfs and dark elves dwell, is deep below the earth. There they work in metals, and are skilful in all smith's work.

So Ull, the god who runs swiftly on snow-shoes, was sent to see what the dwarfs could do. And when the dwarfs had heard his story, they told him that they could make a cord so strong that not even the Asas themselves could break it, and yet to outward seeming so slender that Fenris would not be afraid of trying it. It was to be wrought of six things, the sound of a cat's footsteps, the roots of a mountain, and a fish's breath being amongst them.

And the dwarfs set to work, and twined and twisted the materials so deftly, that none could see the joining, or guess of what woof they were woven. And when the cord was finished, they gave it to Ull, who quickly departed with it for Asgard.

The gods were a little disappointed when they saw so slender a bond, which looked as if it might be easily snapped, but when they had tried their utmost strength upon it, they found that even Thor could do no more than strain it slightly. And in very good spirits, they went to Fenris, and took him with them to the island of Syngvi, in the lake Amsvartnir.

There they feasted, and made merry, and at last began to try feats of strength. One after another broke mighty bars of iron, and rent huge chains in pieces, or hurled stones of prodigious weight.

Fenris followed their example. One crunch of his jaws shivered the strongest iron, and a stroke of his paw sundered the heaviest chains. And when the gods thought he must be somewhat tired, they showed him the rope.

'It is so late in the day,' said Bragi, 'that we will give you no hard task. We have kept the most slender cord until the last. You shall have the first try at it.'

Certainly the cord was very fragile to look at ; but Fenris was wary, he suspected treachery, and at first refused to be bound with it. But the gods

laughed at his fears and said that he was becoming
a coward.

'No coward am I,' replied Fenris, 'but I fear
that ye are playing me false. Let Tyr put his hand
into my mouth as a pledge of your good faith,
then will I submit to be bound.'

So Tyr put his hand into Fenris's mouth, and the
gods wound the rope Gleipner round and round the
wolf's body, and fastened his legs in such a manner
that if the rope were as strong as the dwarfs had
promised, there would be no doubt of his being
their prisoner.

Fenris lay quite still whilst the rope was being
tied, for he had Tyr in his power, and he trusted to
that in case there should be any treachery.

Tyr finding that Fenris was fast bound, at-
tempted gently to withdraw his hand ; but the wolf
kept a firm hold, nor did he loose it even in the
midst of his struggles to break the rope.

The Asi gave a shout. 'Long live the dwarfs
of the Black Elfland, their work is to be trusted.'

And again Fenris strove with all his might to
free himself from his bonds, but in vain, and he lay
on the ground panting and well-nigh exhausted with
his efforts. Tyr's hand was still between his teeth,

and he glared savagely as much as to say, ' We are captives together.'

Then Tyr began to try what force might do, and with the hand that was free he sought to open the wolf's jaws so as to free the other. He had half succeeded when Fenris, in fear lest he might lose it, made a sudden snap and bit it off, and Tyr stood clear of the wolf, but with only one hand.

Fenris was captive now.

And the Asi raised a shout of joy.

Tyr however was silent, sorrowing over his loss, and yet, perhaps, he felt that it was well to get rid of the monster even at such a cost.

Then the Asi bound Fenris to a huge rock, and to fasten him the better they drove a sword through his jaws and pinned him fast.

He howled dreadfully and foam issued from his nostrils. And there he must lie until the day of Ragnaröck, when he, as well as Jormungand, shall once more be free. Then terrible things shall come to pass. But the gods hope that that day is far off, for when it comes they must die.

Three winters without a summer shall go before it, and on the plains of Vigrid, a hundred miles square, a fearful battle shall be fought in which all shall perish.

The gods, the giants, the living and the dead shall all be present at it. The heroes who are dwelling in Odin's halls shall issue forth when they hear the gold-combed cock. The dead who inhabit Hela's dreary dwellings shall come forth when the red cock crows in hell. Jormungand the serpent and Fenris will be unloosed, and Odin and Thor meet their death as it had been foretold.

The gods care not to think of Ragnaröck. Though it must come, they put all thoughts of it away ; and perchance they look beyond to the new earth that is promised them, when the world in which they now dwell shall have been destroyed, and to the time when the gods shall wake up after their death-sleep and live for ever in joy and gladness.

X.

THE STORY OF IDUNA.

ODIN STARTS ON A JOURNEY.

ALTHOUGH Asgard was very beautiful, the Asi did not care always to remain at home. They were fond of travelling abroad to see the rest of the world and to do great things. Even Odin himself got tired of sitting day after day upon his golden throne and holding councils of the gods in the great hall of Valhalla.

Odin liked change as well as any of the Asi. And one day he and Hænir and Loki set off together upon a journey.

As long as they were in the land of Asgard everything was pleasant enough. The grass was soft under their feet ; the fruit was plentiful on the trees ; and there were boars, and deer, and birds innumerable for them to shoot when they needed food. But when they left the bounds of their own land all was changed. Instead of fertile valleys and hills covered with verdure, they found sandy plains on which no shrub would grow, and where there were no refreshing wells of water. Further on they met with barren mountains whose rocky sides were sharp and steep, and in the flinty valleys at their base rolled rivers of water so salt that the least drop gave them unquenchable thirst, so that Odin, Hænir, and Loki could not even moisten their parched throats.

This was not very cheering ; but the travellers kept up their spirits, hoping in time to find the wonderful land, beautiful as Asgard itself, which Loki had told them lay beyond this dismal region. And although Odin did not place much trust in Loki's words, he nevertheless thought it likely that they must in time come to something less desolate than the land through which they were passing, and so he journeyed hopefully along.

Presently he saw what he had hoped for. As they reached the top of a low range of hills, they came in sight of a patch of green pasture-land through which a stream wound peacefully. Here were countless cattle grazing, and the sight cheered Odin and his companions as they had had nothing to eat for some time, for the food which they had brought in their wallets from Asgard they had long since devoured.

Eagerly they killed one of the oxen; and as Loki said that he would make it ready for supper, since he knew more about such things than either Odin or Hænir, it was agreed that he should be left under a wide-spreading tree, and that the other gods should stroll forth and see the beautiful valley which they had happily found.

LOKI'S ADVENTURE WITH THE EAGLE.

There was nothing that Loki liked better than being left to his own devices, and having everything his own way. So no sooner were Odin and Hænir gone than he gathered and lighted a pile of sticks and dry leaves, and soon had a fire hot enough to roast the largest ox that ever lived.

Next he made a spit, for Loki was a crafty god, and fastening the ox to it, he went on cooking, constantly heaping up fresh fuel on the fire, and so keeping up such a heat that none but Loki himself would have cared to be so near to it.

In due time the ox was roasted, or at least Loki thought that it was roasted, for the outside looked as if it were thoroughly well cooked; but when he cut off a small slice and tasted it, he found that it was as raw as when he had fastened it to the spit. Again he set to work, and piling twice as much wood on the fire as he had done at first, he sat down and waited; but he waited in vain—the ox would not roast.

Loki was very much astonished; he had never met with such an ox before, and he did not at all know what to do. He pushed it nearer the fire, indeed the flames were playing close around it, yet they seemed to do nothing. He thought that he must give up his task in despair, when a voice said from among the branches overhead, 'So you can't roast your ox, Loki.' Loki looked up.

'Ah I thought something must be at work somewhere,' said he; 'no, I cannot.'

'If you will promise to give me part of it,' continued the voice, 'I will promise that it shall be cooked in half the time that you have been about it.'

Again Loki looked up, and this time he saw a huge eagle perched upon the topmost branches of the tree. He was so large that his wings stretched all across it, and his eyes looked like two fires shining down upon Loki.

'I wonder that I did not see you before, for you

are large enough,' said Loki. 'Well, as I cannot
cook my supper without your help, I suppose I
must make terms. Yes, you shall have part of it.'

'Very well,' said the eagle, 'I am very hungry,
and I will keep my eye upon it for you.'

Now, whether it was that the eagle's eyes were
really fires as they seemed to be, or whether his
great wings fanned the flames until they rose as
high as the tree itself, it is impossible to say. Whatever the cause might be, in a very few minutes the
ox was ready to be eaten.

'And now for my share,' quoth the eagle. And
coming down from the tree, he planted his claws
firmly in the shoulders of the animal, and said that
he would take them as his portion.

Whereupon Loki grew very angry. He and his
comrades had killed the ox, and he had skinned it,
and had made up the fire, and had been at the
trouble of cooking it, and it was not fair that the
eagle should claim so large a share.

'Where would your cooking have been if I had
not helped you?' asked the eagle.

'There would have been nothing to cook if we
had not found the food,' answered Loki.

'Might makes right,' said the Eagle, wrenching

away the shoulders from the rest of the body. But Loki was not going to give way to him without a struggle, so seizing a great faggot that was lying near, he struck valiantly at the eagle.

'We'll have a fight for it,' said Loki.

'But not here,' answered the eagle.

And lo, to Loki's amazement, he found that one end of the faggot was firmly stuck to the back of the eagle, whilst the other had so grown to his hand that he could not loose his grasp of it.

'Now then,' said the eagle, and up he rose into the air carrying Loki with him. Away they flew, over mountain, over valley, over sea and sandy plain, away! away! away! It was no use for Loki to shout. 'Stop! stop!' which he did with all his might; the eagle had no thought of stopping, and Loki was dragged along until he thought that his arm would be broken.

Sometimes the eagle flew low, and then Loki was bruised against the sharp flinty rocks, or blinded with the dust, or dipped into the sea. Sometimes the eagle flew high, and then Loki was smothered among the clouds, or knocked about amongst myriads of hailstones; and once he thought he was going to be dashed against the stars; and all the time he felt so dizzy, that he feared he was losing his senses altogether.

Once, too, he thought that far, far away he saw the glittering palace of Gladsheim, shining like a gem in Asgard. Then he shouted as loud as he could to one god after another, Odin! Thor! Vidar! Tyr! Heimdall! Bragi! hoping that some might hear him. But no one heeded him.

'Bragi,' said the eagle, slackening his pace a little, 'Bragi. He is the husband of Iduna?'

'Yes,' stammered Loki, almost breathless.

'Well, it is of no use calling upon any of the Asi to help you,' said the eagle, 'but you can help yourself if you choose.'

'How?' asked Loki eagerly.

'I am not an eagle,' said the great bird, pausing in his flight, and settling upon a great thundercloud that was slowly sailing along.

'Are you not?' said Loki, opening his eyes.

'No, I am the Jötun Thiasse, and I have long been in love with Iduna; and if you will take an oath to deliver Iduna and her apples into my hands, I will set you down as near to Asgard as I dare venture.'

Now Loki cared little either for Iduna or Bragi.

Indeed, he rather disliked Bragi, who was always
gladdening the Asi by his honeyed words, and was
therefore applauded by them, and the envious Loki
was vexed whenever he heard anyone praised.
Therefore he willingly took the oath, and promised
to bring Iduna and her apples to Thiasse.

Whereupon the eagle, hidden from sight by
the thunder-cloud, dropped Loki gently down
upon the earth, and Loki opening his eyes which
he had closed as he fell, found himself near the
bounds of Asgard.

IDUNA.

Who was fairer in the land of Asgard than
Iduna ? Fresh as the morning, blithesome as the
singing birds, nimble as the young fawn, never-
tiring, never-sorrowing; full of hope, of joy, of
gladness, the everlasting rose in the garden of
gods.

Well might the god of the voice sweet as honey
choose for his queen the maiden who was the
guardian of everlasting youth. Poetry and youth
ever go together, and so the Asi had blessed the
marriage of Bragi with the daughter of Ivalldr.

The dwarf Ivalldr dwelt in caverns beneath the earth, and there he wrought at his craft full cunningly, and many a gift he made for the gods, but his best gift was given to his child Iduna, who like an imprisoned sunbeam had given light to her father's darksome dwelling.

Where could a more skilful workman be found than the dwarf Ivalldr?

Great was the wonder of the gods when they saw the beautifully chased casket of gold which Ivalldr gave to his daughter on her wedding day, greater when they learned that it contained a treasure which made it a right worthy dower for the bride of one of the Asi.

In the casket were golden apples which only Ivalldr knew how to make, and which could bring back youth to the withering limbs of the old; and thus when the Asi felt that they were losing their strength, they had but to taste Iduna's golden apples, and behold they were young again as when the light of the sun had first risen upon them. And there was yet another wonder, for these apples could never fail. No matter how often the Asi ate of them, they still remained as they had been when the dwarf first made them.

Iduna, therefore, was a great goddess, and she would be missed more than anyone in Asgard. If then the Jötun Thiasse could make her his wife and have her golden apples, he might think himself a very lucky giant.

Bragi and Iduna lived in a palace covered with unfading roses. The garden round it was gay with flowers that seemed to have been dipped in the glory of Bifröst, and the birds that sang their ceaseless song by the fountains were like no other birds that fluttered in the groves of Asgard.

Loki had often been in this garden, though Iduna did not care much to see him there, for she never felt sure but that he might mean some mischief.

But Loki knew the way to the garden, and he knew that he should find Iduna there, feeding her doves, or twining up her roses, or gathering great baskets of sweet-scented violets to strew upon the floor of her home. So when he reached Asgard he went at once to the dwelling of the beautiful goddess, and to the garden, where he found her as he thought he should.

'You have soon come back from your travels, Loki,' she said.

Loki nodded his head.

' I had my reasons,' he said. ' I have left Odin and Hænir in the most wonderful land that you can think of. I never saw anything like it, and in one spot that I alone found there is a tree on which apples grow, far more lovely than yours. I was going to gather one, when suddenly the leaves began to shiver and a voice sighed out of the tree, " None but Iduna may gather the fruit I bear." Therefore I hastened home to tell you of it, and now, if you like, I will take you there, and you can fill your casket up to the brim. It will hold a great many more apples than Ivalldr gave you, and it is a pity that it should not be full.'

Iduna listened, and as she listened a great longing to have some of the beautiful apples stole over her.

' I wish Bragi were at home,' she said, ' and then he could go also.'

' You will be there and back before Bragi comes home if you like to go with me. I found out a short cut as I hastened hither, and it makes me laugh to think how near Odin and Hænir are to Asgard though they have no idea of it.'

' I think I will go with you,' said Iduna.

'As you please,' answered Loki carelessly, 'only you must soon make up your mind, for I cannot wait.' And he turned away, as though he were going to leave her.

'Wait one moment, Loki, I must carry this basket of violets into the house.'

'And bring the casket with you so that we may know how many we want to fill it, for I quite forget the size of the apples. I will carry it for you.'

So Iduna brought the casket, and she and Loki glided through the spacious streets and through the great wide gateway out into the pleasant land that lay around.

'Is it far?' asked Iduna.

'Only just across the border,' said Loki; 'you will be well rewarded when you get there.'

But, alas! no sooner were they over the boundary line than down swooped a great eagle, and before Iduna had time to think about anything Loki had lifted her and her casket on its back, and away flew the Jötun Thiasse with his prize, away to dreary Jötunheim.

SORROW IN ASGARD.

When Bragi came home, he asked for Iduna, but no one knew where she was. The servants had last seen her in the garden, and thither went Bragi to seek for her. But she was not there.

The doves drooped their heads as though they would tell a sorrowful tale if they could only speak ; the flowers had already begun to fade ; the butterflies were fluttering feebly over the withering lilies, as though they had not strength to rise into the air.

And as Bragi gazed and wondered what the sight might mean, he happened to glance into the glassy pool in which the golden fishes were wont to play, and behold they had sunk as in a deep sleep to its lowest depths. As he bent over the pool, he saw that his own face had suddenly grown older ; and as he raised his head, he felt that his limbs were weaker, and he could no longer walk upright and firmly as heretofore.

As he passed through the house again, he noticed that a change had come over everyone he met ; everywhere he saw grey hair, and wrinkles, and stooping shoulders. The dogs and cats even

L

had become halt and blind, and nothing anywhere seemed to have any strength left in it.

Out into the street went Bragi, and he met none but aged people tottering along. On to the king's palace, and there he found a bent and worn old woman in the place of the beautiful Friga, and saw Sif weeping over her golden locks which had turned as white as snow.

A blight had fallen upon Asgard; youth had vanished, and age and decay were creeping over everything because Iduna was not there.

'Iduna is lost, is lost! Where is Iduna?'

Such was the wail that greeted Odin as he came back to his royal city. He had turned his steps homeward sooner than he had intended, for as soon as Loki was gone, the green pastures, the cattle, and the flowing river, had vanished also, and Odin and Hænir found themselves in the midst of a flinty region that spread on every side further than eye could see.

No sooner had the king set foot within his own land than he felt a change come over him, and that his strength was ebbing fast away. He had left his palace in the prime of glorious manhood, he came back to it bent and stricken with age. But the change was not in himself alone; all around were suffering likewise.

'Iduna is lost, is lost! Where is Iduna?'

But no answer came to the cry.

At last a feeble trembling form drew near, and spoke: 'I saw Iduna leave the city gates with Loki.'

'Bring Loki hither.'

And Loki, shrivelled up, and looking almost like a skeleton, was brought before the king.

'Tell me, what hast thou done?' said Odin in a hollow tone.

But Loki, though he shook with fear, made no answer.

Then Thor, exerting all the strength that still remained to him, caught Loki by the nape of the neck, and tossed him up and down with such right good will that his heels sometimes touched the moon and sometimes the sea. For Loki had shrunk away until he had become as light as a feather.

'Tell me what thou hast done?' again said Odin in a voice more hollow than before, 'tell me, or thou shalt suffer unheard-of tortures, and afterwards shalt be put to death.'

Then Loki fell upon his knees, and in a tremulous tone told of all that had happened to him since Odin and Hænir had left him roasting the ox.

What was to be done ? With Iduna, youth had gone from Asgard, the freshness of life was lost, the ills of mortality were setting in. And not alone did the Asi feel it, but the fruits and flowers, the corn, the vines, the forest trees themselves were dying; the birds had ceased to sing, and the beasts had lain down to die upon the withered herbage.

' If Freyia would lend him her hawk's feather dress, Loki would somehow bring back Iduna.'

So the dress was brought, and Loki slipped it on. He shook the plumage aright, and as he rose in the air, the Asi watched a gallant hawk dart swiftly towards Jötunheim.

They watched and watched until the hawk was but a speck against the sky.

They watched and watched until the speck could no more be seen.

THE RESCUE.

Iduna was sitting upon a rock looking over the great grey sea that plashed drearily upon the barren shores of Jötunheim. Her golden casket was lying in her lap, and she was counting over the apples and thinking upon the treachery of Loki.

She was singing a song in her own language, and Thiasse, who had just put out to sea in his fishing boat, hearing it, paused to listen; and it sent a thrill of joy through his heart. He knew not the words, he only felt how sweet was the voice of the singer.

> For thee my heart is sighing, Asgard mine,
> For thy fair roses, thy eternal springs,
> For my meek snow-white doves that o'er the fount
> Flutter their silver wings.
>
> Oh, would I were a bird; then unto thee
> Upon swift pinions would I wing my flight;
> No storm should hinder me, nor would I fear
> The dark and starless night.
>
> Oh, would I were a wave upon the sea,
> I'd flow and flow until I reached thy shore,
> There plash my song of love at thy dear feet,
> And rest for evermore.
>
> Oh, would I were the northern light, that streams
> In rose-stained flashes o'er the star-lit sky,
> High in the heavens a flaming wreath I'd weave
> To crown thy turrets high.
>
> O, Asgard, Asgard! O ye Asi hear!
> Sad pines Iduna in the land of snow,
> Her tears flow fast, her soul longs for the fields
> Where flowers immortal blow.

And Thiasse, still with the sweet song in his heart, rowed further and further away.

And Iduna began to weep.

Someone else had heard Iduna's song, and this was Loki, who, in the likeness of a hawk, swooped down and perched beside the sorrowing princess.

'So you would like to be a bird,' said he, 'that you might fly away to Asgard ?'

'Loki !' exclaimed Iduna joyfully, for she knew at once who was there.

'Yes, Loki! If you are tired of Jötunheim, I will take you back with me. It is not often that wishers get what they wish for ; but as it was my fault that you came here, it is but fair that I should take you home again.'

'Good Loki !' said Iduna.

'Scarcely that perhaps,' replied Loki; 'nevertheless, I have come upon a good errand. There is great mourning throughout the land of Asgard, and the Asi find that they cannot do without you.'

And Loki could not help chuckling as he thought of the miserable plight the gods were in. 'Have you any choice as to what sort of bird you would like to be ?'

'No,' replied Iduna.

Then she added, 'Perhaps a swallow is the fleetest.'

'Be it so then,' answered Loki. And as he spoke, Iduna vanished, and a swallow rose in the air. Loki seized it in his claws, and away flew the hawk and the swallow through the heavens.

Away! Away! to Asgard.

Surely the flowers knew that Iduna was coming, for they began to raise their drooping heads; a gentle dew stole over the grass, and the tiny blades drank thirstily of it. The white doves that had been sitting with ruffled plumage on the brink of the fountain began to stroke their ruffled feathers. The Asi felt a fresh glow in their veins. Iduna was coming, was coming.

And a flush of hope overspread each grey wrinkled face.

And on, and on flew the hawk and the swallow. They were in sight of Asgard now. Joy! joy! Iduna would see the golden gates and rose-wreathed palaces once more.

Ha! what is that dark cloud looming in the distance, that grows larger and darker as it draws nearer, a dark cloud that has dragged two shining stars from heaven, so it appears to the watching Asi.

As it comes nearer it shapes itself into the form of a bird with fiery eyes and wings outstretched ; they can almost hear the flapping of them as the eagle cleaves the air.

Yes, it is an eagle; it is the Jötun Thiasse, in his eagle's dress, speeding swiftly after the hawk and the swallow. For Thiasse, when he came back from his fishing expedition, found that Iduna was gone, and he was not slow in divining what had happened ; therefore he drew on his feather garb and started in chase of Iduna.

Loki knew him, Iduna knew him, and she trembled. But they held on their flight.

The Asi know him now ; and, lo ! the flowers are drooping again, and a darker look of age and care sits upon the brows of the gods.

Thiasse is gaining upon them, even as the walls of Asgard are close at hand.

' Logs, chips ; heap up a pile as high and higher than the walls ! '

' Higher, higher ! ' so shout the Asi as they work with lusty zeal. And along the outer wall of Asgard a fence of light dry wood is raised.

Then Bragi takes a torch, and in an instant the quick flames crackle through the crisp sticks and chips.

A smoke—a blaze—How will it end? Which will win the race: they who flee or he who follows?

Nay, Loki does not mind the fire; he has darted through it, and the hawk and swallow flutter to the feet of the king.

And the eagle. His heavy wings are fearfully scorched; they bear him up no longer, and down he falls into the devouring flames. The Asi, with loud cries, rush upon their foe and hew him in pieces.

So dies Thiasse.

Then the fire blazed up no longer, the smoke rolled away, the sun shone brightly, and not a cloud was to be seen in the blue skies.

REJOICINGS IN ASGARD.

Iduna stood in the midst of the Asi, and as she gazed upon their altered looks she gave a sigh and then a smile, and, opening her golden casket, she offered her apples to those who cared to taste of them.

The Asi eagerly pressed forward, and, as they tasted, youth, strength and beauty returned to them with renewed glory, and their hearts were filled with thankfulness that life and youth were brought back to Asgard. Loud shouted they with swords unsheathed and waved above their heads: 'All hail, Iduna!'

And at the shout the birds sent forth a burst of song, the waters rippled into life, and rang a silver peal of liquid bells, the roses breathed a richer perfume round, the golden fishes leaped and kissed the crystal wavelets, the weary beasts that had lain down to die upon the withered grass arose and frolicked in the flower-strewn pastures.

Sif combed her golden locks in joyous glee, and Friga in new beauty sought her lord. Heimdall heard the sounds of life and joy with keener ear, and Thor, swinging his hammer, felt that he could conquer a world of giants.

Iduna threw her arms round Bragi's neck, and made him stoop so low that he could hear her softly whisper, 'Perhaps I had never come back to Asgard had not the true Runes of Mimir declared that thy sweet gift of poetry should never die.'

XI.

HOW THOR GOT A CAULDRON FOR AGER,
LORD OF HELSEYIA.

ONCE upon a time, the Jötun Ager, Lord of Helseyia, visited Asgard.

Now there was not much friendship between the
Asi and the giants, for the giants were not to be
trusted, and most of their fine words came to
nothing. However, for some reason or other, the
Asi paid good heed to Ager, and feasted him at a
splendid banquet; and when the Lord of Helseyia
had partaken of the rich fare and of the sparkling
mead, he besought Odin and all the Asi to come and
see him in his own halls, where he would set before
them as good a feast as it was in his power to give.

Eagerly the gods accepted his bidding, for Ager
was a very rich Jötun, and they looked forward to
a feast that should be worth going many miles to
share.

But after the Lord of Helseyia had gone to his
own country, the Asi, hearing nothing more about

the feast, began to suspect that Ager meant to play them false, and in order to find this out they slew a goat, and by looking at its entrails they learnt that Ager had neither cauldron nor kettle of any kind.

Now, if he had no vessels wherein to cook food, how could he make a feast? So the gods said that Ager's bidding did but show yet more the treachery of the giants.

The Asi were very wroth at finding they were likely to be balked, and sent Thor to insist upon Ager's giving them the feast he had promised.

So Thor set off, and found Ager on the sea-shore not far from his castle, where he was just gone to fish. Ager was rather an idle Jötun, and he pre-ferred tossing about in his boat to hunting among the mountains.

He was somewhat surprised at the coming of Thor, and a good deal frightened, for he guessed upon what errand he had come. However, he pretended to be very glad to see him, and invited him to go fishing with him.

'No,' said Thor bluntly, 'I have not time to do that; I must carry back an answer to the message I have brought as speedily as I can.'

'And what may the message be?' asked Ager, inwardly trembling, though he strove to keep up a bold look.

'The Asi have sent to know upon what day they are to sup with you.'

Then Ager began to stammer, and he tried to show how one thing had happened and then another, which had prevented his giving the banquet; but his words became so confused that Thor could make nothing of them, and being a very blunt and straightforward god, he told Ager to leave off talking, and to answer a simple question,

'Are you going to give a feast to the Asi or not?'

It was a question to which only 'yes' or 'no' was needed, but Ager was not ready to give either of these simple answers, so he said: 'How can I have the food cooked if I have not a cauldron large enough? And, what is more, I know not where to get one. Now if you will get one for me, the Asi shall have their banquet without delay.'

It was rather a bold request to make of the great god Thor, but Thor did not seem to be annoyed at it. He had, at any rate, some answer to his question, and he said that he would return to Asgard and take counsel with the Asi about the matter.

II.

The Asi at first thought that they would make war upon Ager, and despoil him of all his wealth for having dared to insult them, by asking them to a feast which he knew himself unable to give.

But Tyr, the son of the Jötun Hymir, one of the most powerful giants in Utgard, stepped forward and said that if a cauldron only were needed, his father had several, each large enough to cook as much food as Ager could possibly require.

'And if Thor will come home with me,' added Tyr, 'I think that with a little craft we shall be able to get one.'

Now Thor was always fond of adventures, and as the Jötun Hymir was mightier in every way than the Lord of Helseyia, he thought that, if there should be any fighting to do, the giant of Utgard would be the worthier foe.

Therefore, taking Tyr with him, he mounted his chariot, and they sped quickly along on their way to Utgard.

As the goat knew every turn of the road, Thor had only to let the reins lie loose and to amuse himself with looking at the country as they passed along. Not that he had much time for that either, for so fleet was the goat's pace, that Thor and Tyr seemed scarcely to have passed the great gates of Asgard, when they found themselves close to the city of the giants.

Thor remembered it well enough, and how he and Loki and Thialfe had crept between the bars. But it did not seem so high now, for there was no magical power at work ; and though there were huge giants walking about the streets, Thor was tall himself, and did not look so very small among them.

They passed by the city, and journeyed on some leagues further into the country, until they came to a great castle, that looked dreary enough amongst the barren mountains.

'This is my father's castle,' said Tyr ; 'it is one of the strongest in Utgard.'

And so it was. It was hewn out of the solid rock, the walls were twenty feet thick, the door was of massive iron, the windows were mere loop holes, and it looked altogether more like a prison than like the home of a mighty giant.

Tyr rang the bell, and a face cautiously peered through a grating.

Seeing Tyr, the face disappeared, the door opened, and Thor and his companion entered.

The passage was dark, and the great hall, which they reached after climbing up a steep flight of stairs, would have been dark also, had it not been for a clumsy lamp that hung from the ceiling, for daylight could scarcely come through the small windows.

Here they were met by Tyr's grandmother, a wonderful person with nine hundred heads. Thor found it very perplexing to know which to look at, for she nodded first with one head then with another, she spoke first with one tongue then with another, then with several together, which was very confusing. She also winked her eyes so quickly, that she made Thor wink also, until the tears stood in his eyes. Her hearing, as we may suppose, was very sharp, when she could give a separate ear to eighteen hundred sounds at once. Thor could not tell how all these heads were placed upon one neck, and as, with all his striving, he could not understand it, he had to rest content with the fact that it was so.

After her came Tyr's mother, who was a fair-haired beautiful woman. Standing by Thor's hideous grandmother, she seemed perhaps more beautiful than she really was.

Tyr's mother brought to Thor a welcome-cup, and was very glad to see Tyr, who had been away for some time.

'But I fear that my husband will not give you a hearty greeting,' she said to Thor, 'for he often comes home in a very bad temper, and then woe betide the first on whom he vents his wrath. You had better therefore let me hide you until his anger is a little cooled.' Tyr was willing to do this cheerfully, for he knew what his father was; but Thor was ashamed to skulk. Nevertheless, he thought, 'the wife knows the ways of the household better than I do, and it may be better to follow her counsel.'

Then Tyr's mother pointed to some huge kettles or cauldrons; in fact, the very cauldrons of which Tyr had spoken. They were fastened to a great pillar at one end of the hall, and made a screen large enough to hide a troop of soldiers. 'There,' she said, 'if you and Tyr will get behind them, you will be hidden very safely.'

So Thor and Tyr crept under the cauldrons, and there she left them,—Thor's heart swelling with shame, and burning to show Hymir and his wife what a mighty god he was.

III.

After a time, a great roaring and bellowing was heard outside.

'It is my father,' whispered Tyr, 'calling to the dogs.'

As the noise died down a little, Thor felt the house begin to shake, and great crashes were heard from time to time, so that Thor thought the roof must be falling in.

'It is my father coming up stairs,' explained Tyr; 'he is a little noisy.'

'Oh,' said Thor.

Then the door of the hall was flung open, and Thor thought that a whirlwind had swept into the room, for everything clattered, and shivered, and seemed to be banging about; the table creaked and groaned, and the lamp almost went out.

But Tyr whispered, 'It is only my father kicking off his hunting boots.'

'Oh,' again answered Thor; and he peeped out from his hiding-place, and saw the huge giant standing in the middle of the room.

He was so tall that his head touched the ceiling, and his hair was like a waggon load of sheep's wool, all ropy and tangled, his thick beard like a frozen forest, whilst his eyes seemed almost as large as his mother's nine hundred pairs put together, and his voice sounded like the bellowing of a herd of cattle.

Truly he was a very terrible giant to look at, and, for a moment, Thor himself was glad of the shelter of the cauldrons.

Hymir's gentle wife stood beside him, and Thor could not help wondering what had made her fall in love with him.

However, she seemed not to mind his rough ways, and she persuaded him to sit down and listen to what she had to tell him.

'Rejoice with me, Hymir,' she said, 'for great happiness has befallen us. Our son, our long-lost Tyr, has come home from his travels, and with him he brings the noble Veorr, sprung from a gentle race.'

'I see them not,' answered the giant; 'why are they not here to greet me?'

'Nay,' replied his wife, 'they are not far off, but no sooner did they hear thy voice chiding the hounds than they hid themselves, fearing to meet thine anger. Behind yon pillar, whereon the cauldrons hang, stand Veorr and thy son.'

Then the giant cast so savage a glance at the pillar, and on the ceiling above it, that, unable to bear his look, the beams split asunder, and the heavy pillar shook.

Then the giant cast a still more savage glance upon the eight cauldrons, which fell to the ground with a fearful crash that well nigh deafened Thor and Tyr.

Seven of the cauldrons were broken to pieces, but the eighth, which was the largest, was not hurt.

When the cloud of dust had cleared away, Tyr and his friend stepped forth from behind the pillar.

The giant did not seem overjoyed to see them.

'A pretty pair, hiding away like mice,' he said scornfully; then looking more closely at Thor, he started. 'The god Thor!' he exclaimed, for he knew his old enemy.

Thor was not altogether at his ease, for he remembered how mighty a giant Hymir was, and the breaking of the cauldrons had not cheered him. If the glance of Hymir could do such things, what might not his arm do?

However, he spoke as though he was well pleased

to see the Jötun, and said that Tyr, who had been sojourning awhile in Asgard, had persuaded him to visit Utgard.

'I had no notion you had such fine castles in your country,' added Thor, trying to say something pleasant.

'They are strong,' said the giant, looking round his great dreary hall. 'I don't know that they are handsome. I think not, but they're good enough for me. Wife,' said he, turning suddenly round, 'where is my supper?'

She whispered something to him.

'Not enough?' said he aloud. 'Make it enough then, since the god Thor has come to visit us. Have three oxen slain and dressed at once. I have had a hard day's hunting, and I am hungry.'

So Hymir's wife went away, and very soon the three oxen roasted whole were brought in on a mighty dish.

Hymir, willing to make Thor believe that he needed a great deal of food, ate two of them, and Tyr shared the third with Thor.

The giant's wife grieved sadly to see so much food taken. What were they to do if it should go on?

' Never mind,' said Thor, ' I can row a boat, and I can fish, and to-morrow I will go out to sea and bring home fish in plenty, if your husband will only give me some bait.'

To this Hymir agreed.

' Let Thor go into the pastures and take what bait he pleases,' said he.

IV.

The next morning Thor rose early, and told Hymir that he would go and fish.

' A bull's head,' said he, ' is the best bait that I know of, and with that alone will I fish.'

Hymir wondered at his words, but he said nothing, and waited to see what Thor would do.

Thor went into the fields where was a drove of fierce cattle grazing ; he walked fearlessly in among them, and seizing a large black bull by the horns, dealt it so heavy a blow with his hammer that it fell down dead on the spot, and then, with one jerk of his hand, he twisted off its head.

' You surprise me,' said Hymir.

And they went down to the boat together.

They got in, and Thor, taking the oars, made one

HOW THOR GOT A CAULDRON.

*'Thor went into the fields where was a drove of fierce
cattle grazing'* (p. 166).

or two strokes, which carried them many leagues out to sea. Hymir, however, said nothing; he was waxing wroth and envious, for he marvelled at the strength of his guest, and longed to be able to show that his own might was greater.

Thor was using all his strength, for he was very eager that Hymir should see how great his powers were. Neither spoke, but from time to time each looked askance at the other.

Hymir was the first to throw out his line, and, hiding his fears, he half closed his eyes and waited for a bite.

Soon he felt a heavy pull at the line, and, drawing it carefully in, he found that he had hooked a tremendous whale.

He took it off the hook, and threw it into the bottom of the boat as though he caught whales every day.

It was Thor's turn now to try his luck.

He fixed the bull's head to the hook, and cast it into the water.

Then he waited, for he knew that what he angled for would be longer in coming up than the whale. But he did not wait in vain. Presently he knew by the shock that the boat received that the great serpent of Midgard had fastened on the bait.

Then began a fierce struggle ; the serpent struggling to get free, and Thor striving, with might and main, to bring the monster to the surface of the water. The sea began to heave and roll as though a storm had arisen, and the great heavy-built boat tossed as though it had been but a cockleshell, and it was all that the Jötun Hymir could do to prevent being dashed out.

Still the struggle went on ; now Thor had almost drawn the monster to the side of the boat, now he was almost dragged into the water himself by the sudden plunges of his wriggling enemy. At last, after a fierce strife, Thor dragged up the serpent's wolfish head on a level with the boat, whilst fold after fold of his shiny body lay for leagues upon the water.

The Jötun Hymir almost turned to stone with fear at the sight of the monster, which glared hideously with its cruel eyes, and poured forth streams of venomous vapour from its nostrils.

When he had held it long enough to show that he had indeed caught his prize, Thor gave the serpent a heavy blow with his hammer, whilst the earth shook with fear, and the mountains groaned; then, rising up, with his whole strength he hurled the monster into the watery world again. And down sank the serpent of Midgard once more to the lowest depths of the ocean.

Hymir might well think it hopeless to do a greater feat than Thor had done, and he sat sulkily in the stern of the boat, leaving Thor to row the whole of the way home.

Thor, however, was so well pleased that he plied the oars cheerfully, and when, as they came near the landing-place, Hymir asked him to help in hauling up the boat on shore, and in carrying home their prize, Thor plunged into the water, and, taking up the boat, threw it, whale, oars, benches, ropes, and all, upon his shoulders and carried it up to the giant's castle.

Hymir's wife was glad to see the whale; it would surely give food for some days, and she was going to cut it up, when Hymir, in an angry tone, bade her cook it whole.

'Our guest has tired himself to-day,' he said.

'That have I not,' answered Thor. 'I am as fresh as when I set out this morning.'

But the Jötun pretended not to believe it.

'Well,' said he, 'we will try your strength after supper; not now, for at present I am too sleepy to look after anything.'

And Hymir closed his eyes, not that he was really sleepy; he was only very much vexed, and he did not want to talk to Thor. He wished also to think of some trial of strength in which Thor would be likely to fail, for it would never do to let him return to Asgard triumphing over the great Jötun Hymir.

V.

The whale was served up for supper with a sauce of which the giant was very fond. This put him in rather a better mood. The ale was also very good, for Hymir's mother had brought her eighteen hundred eyes to see after the brewing of it.

This warmed the Jötun's heart, and made him feel twice the giant that he was before supper.

'And now,' said he to Thor, 'if you can in one trial dash my drinking-bowl in pieces, I will own that you are mightier than I.'

Thor laughed, and without moving from his seat, he raised his hand and struck a granite pillar that was near him with such force that he broke it in two.

'If I can do that,' he said, 'I can break a drinking-cup.'

'Pooh,' replied the giant, 'that is nothing. My drinking-bowl is harder than iron.'

The servants, at a sign from Hymir, placed the bowl upon the ground before Thor.

'Lift it,' said the giant. It was much heavier than Thor had thought, and the Jötun was much delighted at seeing that Thor had been cheated by its look.

'Throw it,' he said.

Now Hymir's wife was standing near to Thor, and, pretending to be busy with the dishes on the table, she bent down so that her husband could not see her lips move, and she whispered, 'Throw it against Hymir's head.'

Thor did as she bade him. With all his might he dashed the bowl against the giant's skull, and the bowl fell to the ground in pieces, whilst the Jötun remained unhurt.

Then Thor stood on his guard, for he thought that the giant would be fiercely wroth. But Hymir was too much taken up in grieving over his broken bowl, which no one yet had been able to break.

Besides, Thor had proved himself more subtle and skilful than he had thought to find him.

He only said, 'Thor has taken too much ale.'

After which he proposed that Thor and Tyr should try to lift the heavy cauldron that remained unbroken.

Twice Tyr strove to do so, and twice he failed ; but when it came to Thor's turn, not only did he lift it, but he placed it on his head, and, darting through the door, down the stairs, and along the hall, he gained the outer gate, and fled away with the cauldron as fast as he could go.

Up sprang Hymir, but his feet were unsteady, and the ale was making him feel drowsy. Nevertheless, he roused himself as well as he could, and hastened after Thor, calling, as he sped along, upon the other Jötuns to join in the chase.

VI.

By this time, Thor was many leagues off, but he was quite out of breath with running so fast and so far, and he stopped for awhile to rest.

Presently he heard the shouts of the giants in the distance, and so he took to flight again, but the weight of the cauldron was so great that he could not go as fast as before, and the giants gained upon him.

Thor could hear them near him, and he at once made up his mind what to do.

The great god Thor must not be seen running away from his enemies ; therefore he stopped, and placing the cauldron on the ground, he brandished his hammer and waited for the foe.

Up came the troop of giants, with Hymir at their head, and the fight began. It seemed to be an unequal one, but then Thor was the strongest of the Asi, and if he could conquer the serpent of Midgard he could surely defend himself against the giants.

And so he did. And, moreover, so well did he aim the blows of his hammer, that, after a short and sharp fight, the giants lay dead upon the field of battle, and Thor, raising the cauldron once more upon his head, bore it off in triumph to Asgard.

VII.

When Thor had thus got for the Lord of Helseyia a cauldron large enough to hold everything that he could need, Ager could no longer delay to make the feast which he had said that he would give to the Asi.

So when all things were ready, Ager sent out to bid the gods and goddesses, and Loki, too, was bidden among the guests.

It was a splendid feast; the hall was lighted with gold till it gleamed like the sun. The dishes and goblets moved about just as the guests wanted them. Hands which they could not see poured out the wine and placed the rarest fruits before the Asi.

Besides this, Ager had two servants who served the guests so well that all the gods praised them loudly; but Loki was so envious that he slew one of the servants, whose name was Fimassenger. Then the Asi rose in a body, but when they had thrust Loki out of the hall, they sat down again to carouse, and all said that never was a better feast than this which the Lord of Helseyia had given to them.

Thor alone of all the Asi was not there. He was journeying in the east, and perhaps he was doing feats as mighty as those which he wrought when · he was seeking to get the cauldron for the Jötun Ager.

XII.

KING OLAF THE SAINT.

HUNDREDS of years ago lived Olaf, a brave king, and his brother Harald Haardrade.

One day, when these brothers were talking together, they began to speak of old Norroway, the land of their birth.

' It is a land full of high hills,' said one.

' It is a land full of fertile valleys,' said the other, 'where there is no lack of waving corn, fair pastures, and summer flowers.'

' It is a land over which anyone might be content to reign,' said Olaf; 'a monarch might be justly proud of such a kingdom.'

' Truly,' replied Harald Haardrade; ' better fortune could no man wish.'

' Then,' answered Olaf, ' let us make a bargain. Our ships are in the harbour; they are well matched. Let us sail forth, and he who reaches first our native land, shall be king of old Norroway.'

' I am quite willing,' said Harald Haardrade;

'yet there is one condition I should like to make. Thou hast said that our ships are equally matched; nevertheless, I take thine to be the fastest sailer. Art thou willing to change vessels with me? So will we run the race.'

'I am willing,' said Olaf. 'If thou thinkest my vessel to be the fleeter, take her, and welcome, and I will take thine. Is this a fair bargain?'

'Perfectly fair,' answered Harald Haardrade, well satisfied that he should have his brother's ship.

Now the vessel belonging to Olaf was called the Dragon. Lightly she danced over the waves, and a child could have turned her north, south, east, or west, by just one touch to the rudder. Harald Haardrade's ship, the Ox, was heavier built, and not so easy to manage; nevertheless, there was no fault to be found with her.

However, Olaf thought one vessel as good as the other, and, therefore, said nought against his brother's proposal; perhaps, too, he felt himself to be the better seaman. However, this may have been, the story does not say; but there is reason to think that something in his heart told Olaf that the change of ships would make no difference to their captains.

N

So the brothers parted, and Olaf, having made all things ready, went to the church to pray for a blessing upon his work, 'For,' said he, 'how can I expect to prosper unless I have the blessing of heaven?'

And as he passed along the aisle of the stately building, with his beautiful hair flowing over his shoulders, the people wished him success, and prayed that good King Olaf might win the race.

As he moved along in solemn mood, a messenger came in hot haste, and stopped him, saying, 'Why dost thou waste the time, King Olaf? thy brother is sailing away in the Dragon. Far ahead of thee will he be, if thou dost not turn thy steps aside from the altar, and follow him without delay.'

But King Olaf answered the messenger, 'Let those sail who choose to sail; I will not depart without the blessing of heaven.'

And so he waited quietly until the mass was over, and then went calmly down to the seashore.

The great white-crested waves were dashing on the strand, and the Ox rocked heavily at her moorings, and over the wide sweep of blue sea there was no sign of the Dragon. Away, far away,

had the Dragon sped; the wind was in her favour,
and she had weighed anchor, and set her sails, and
danced gallantly away till there were now many
miles between her and the shore. Olaf strained
his eyes, and saw a speck of white that fluttered for
a moment and then vanished. Perchance it might
be the Dragon.

However, Olaf did not despair. He had asked
the blessing of heaven upon his undertaking, and
although the beginning seemed bad, yet he said in
his heart, 'Who can see so far as the end? I will
not be dismayed.'

Strong in the might of his faith, he bade the
sailors get ready, and when all was done he stepped
on board his vessel. The anchor was raised; a
gentle breeze stirred the sails; the helmsman
guided the ship seaward; and as King Olaf stood
at the prow, he said reverently, 'O Ox, Ox,
speed thee on in the Name of the Lord.'

Then he leaned forward, and taking hold of one
of the white horns of the Ox, as though it had
been a living creature, he said, 'Now speed thee, O
thou patient Ox, even as though thou wert going
to pasture in fragrant clover fields.'

And as if in answer to his words, the heavy

vessel gave a leap, and gallantly ploughed thê wild waves. And the white spray rose even until it frosted over the king's beautiful locks, and he shouted to the watcher on the topmost mast, 'Ho, lad ! Ho! Can'st thou see aught of the fleet-sailing Dragon ?'

And the lad answered, 'I see naught upon the sea. There is not even a fishing-boat out upon the broad waters.'

And on they sailed in silence. After awhile, King Olaf called to the lad again, 'Ho, lad ! Ho! Can'st thou see aught of the good ship Dragon?'

Then the lad answered, 'Nigh the land of Norroway I espy the silken sails of a vessel. The sun shines upon them, and they glitter as though they were bordered with gold.'

And King Olaf knew that it was his own brave ship, and again they sailed on in silence.

After awhile he called yet again to the lad, 'Ho, lad ! Ho! Can'st thou see aught of the Dragon?'

And the lad made answer, 'Nigh the shores of old Norroway, under the shade of the purple mountains, I see a vessel riding full sail before the wind, and I know that it is the good ship Dragon.'

Then King Olaf struck the Ox upon the ribs, and cried, 'Faster, faster, thou Ox, faster. There is no time to lose.'

And again he struck the Ox upon the eye, and shouted, ' Faster, faster, faster, if thou would'st have me win the haven.'

And suddenly it seemed as though the Ox had started into life, and was putting forth all its new-gained powers, for forward bounded the vessel with a sudden leap. Swiftly, swiftly, swiftly, no one had ever known such sailing. Swifter than a bird on the wing, swifter than an arrow through the air. So sped the Ox through the foaming sea. The sailors could not climb the rigging; indeed, it was more than they could do to stand firmly upon the deck ; so King Olaf lashed them firmly to the masts, though the steersman asked him who was going to guide the ship. ' I will see to that myself,' answered King Olaf ; ' not one of you shall be lost through me. I will guide the ship straight on like a line of light.'

And King Olaf stood by the helm, and he steered neither to the right nor to the left, but on, straight on, and his eye was fixed upon the goal.

'So must I run,' he said, 'if I would win the race.'

What mattered it to King Olaf though rocks and mountains stood in the way ? His faith was stronger than the rocks. Right onward he went, and the valleys filled with water, and the mountains disappeared, the blue waves rolled over them, and the Ox went triumphantly on its way.

Out came running the little elves, for the sudden rising of the floods had disturbed them.

'Who art thou, bold mariner, who sailest over our homes ? Behold the mountains shake with fury. Tell us what is thy name ?'

'Quiet ye, quiet ye, little people,' answered King Olaf. 'I am Saint Olaf; turn ye into stones until I come this way again.'

So the little elves turned into stones, and rolled down the mountain sides, and the good ship went on her way.

She had not gone far before out came an old Carline, and said, 'Saint Olaf, I know you, with your beard shining like red gold. Wherefore do you bring with you the waters to mock us in our dwellings ? Your ship has burst through the wall of my chamber. Evil luck be with you.'

KING OLAF THE SAINT.

'Out came running the little elves' (p. 182).

Then Saint Olaf, for he was a saint as well as a king, fixed his glance witheringly upon the old Carline.

'Be thou turned into a flint rock,' said he, 'and so remain for ever and ever.'

And the Carline was turned into a rock, and Saint Olaf and his crew sailed on and on.

So fleetly flew the good ship Ox, that anyone must have had good eyes to see her as she flashed past, for so she sped on that if Saint Olaf drew his bow and shot an arrow forward, it fell far behind in the wake of the vessel.

This was fast sailing indeed, and with such speed it is not wonderful that though Harald Haardrade had had the start of his brother, yet Saint Olaf reached home three days before him.

Harald Haardrade was wild with rage when he came those three days later and found Saint Olaf king of Norroway.

And he raged and raged until at length he became a dragon. And this is the last that we hear of Harald Haardrade.

Now, as Saint Olaf had prayed for the blessing of heaven before he set out on his voyage, it was natural that his first act upon landing should be to go to the nearest church to return thanks for having so mightily prospered.

And as he walked up the crowded nave, a golden glory beamed from his fair hair, and the people of Norroway learned a great lesson from the faith of King Olaf the Saint.

XIII.

THE STORY OF FRITHIOF.

I.

In a cottage overshadowed by wide spreading oaks, and surrounded by a garden in which bloomed the sweetest flowers of summer, lived an aged peasant named Hilding.

Two children might be seen playing about the garden from sunrise to sunset, but they were not old Hilding's children. The handsome boy was the son of the Thane, Thorsten Vikingsson; the little girl, with dovelike eyes and silken tresses, was the daughter of good King Belé.

Together the little ones played through the long pleasant days in their foster-father's garden, or wandered through the woods, or climbed the hills that sheltered them from the northern winds. The boy would seek treasures from the birds' nests for his fair companion, not even fearing to rob the mountain eagle, so that he might bring the spoil to Ingebjorg. He would also take her far out on the blue sea in his little boat, and Ingebjorg never felt afraid as long as Frithiof was with her.

As Frithiof grew older, he became a great hunter, and once he slew without weapons a fierce bear, which he brought home in triumph and laid at Ingebjorg's feet.

During the winter evenings, they sat by the blazing logs on the hearth, and Hilding told them wonderful stories of Asgard and all its glories, of Odin the king of the gods, and of the beautiful Friga.

But Frithiof thought she could not be half so beautiful as Ingebjorg. And once he said so to her, and it pleased her exceedingly. And he said, moreover, that when he was a man, Ingebjorg should be his wife. This also she was glad to hear, for she loved Frithiof better than anyone in the world.

But old Hilding told them not to talk nonsense, for Ingebjorg was a king's daughter, and Frithiof but the son of a Thane.

II.

In a room of his palace stood King Belé. He was leaning on his sword, musing over all that was past, and thinking of the future. He was an old man, and he felt that his strength was failing him.

With him was his faithful friend Thorsten Vikingsson. They had grown up to manhood together, they had fought in many a battle side by side. They had been companions at many a feast and revel, and now, when old age had fallen upon them, they drew closer to one another, feeling that the hand of death was raised to summon them into another world.

'The end of life is near,' said the king, 'the shadow of death is cast upon me. No longer do I care for all that men call pleasure. The chase hath lost its charm, the helmet sits heavy upon my brow, and the mead hath lost its flavour. I would that my sons were here so that I might give them my blessing.'

Then the servants summoned to King Belé's presence his two sons Helgi and Halfdan. Dark was the countenance of Helgi, and there was blood upon his hands, for he had just been assisting at the mid-day sacrifice. But the face of Halfdan was bright as the early morning, and he was as light and joyous as his brother was dark and gloomy.

Frithiof also came, for the Thane Thorsten Vikingsson desired to see him, that he too might bless his son when King Belé blessed the royal princes.

And the two old friends spoke words of wisdom to their children, and prayed that the gods might be with them in peace and war, in joy and sorrow, and grant them a long life and a glorious death.

And when their counsels and prayers were ended, King Belé said, 'And now, O sons, I bid you remember, in that day when death shall claim me and my faithful friend, that ye lay our bones side by side near the shore of the great ocean.'

III.

In due time, King Belé died, and Helgi and Halfdan shared his kingdom between them.

Thorsten Vikingsson died also, and Frithiof became lord of his ancestral home of Framnäs.

Rich treasures did that home contain, three of them of magic power.

The first was the sword of Angurvadel. Blood-red it shone in time of war, and woe to him who contended with its owner on the battle-field.

Next was an arm-ring of pure gold, made by the god Völund, and given by him to one of Thorsten Vikingsson's forefathers. Once it was stolen and carried to England by the Viking Soté, but Thorsten and his friend King Belé pursued the robber. Over the sea they sailed after the Viking, and landed at a lonely place where the rocks reared up their sharp points and made the coast dangerous.

There were deep caverns which the waters filled when the tide was up, so lone and dark that men were almost afraid to go into them.

But Thorsten Vikingsson and the king his master were not daunted. Hither had they come after the pirate, and here it was that he had last been heard of, and they searched along the shore and in the caves, and peered into every hole and cranny until their eyes grew strained and heavy, but no Viking Soté was to be seen.

They had almost given up hope of finding him, when, looking through a chink that had hitherto escaped their notice, a fearful sight was seen by the valiant Thane.

Within a mighty vault, forming a still cold tomb, there lay a vessel all complete, with masts and spars and anchor; and on the deck there sat a grim skeleton clad in a robe of flame, and on his skinless arm glittered the golden arm-ring wrought by Völund. The figure held in his left hand a blood-stained sword, from which he was trying to scour away the stains.

'It is my arm-ring,' said Thorsten Vikingsson ; 'it is the spirit of the Viking Soté.'

And forthwith he forced his way into the tomb, and, after a deadly conflict with the spectre, regained his treasure.

And the two friends sailed home in triumph.

The third great thing that Frithiof inherited was the dragon-ship Ellide, which his forefathers had won in the following manner :—

One of them, a rough rude Viking, with a tender heart, was out at sea, and on a wreck that was fast sinking saw an old man with green locks sitting disconsolately.

The good-natured Viking picked him up, took him home, gave him of the best of food and of sparkling mead, and would have lodged him in his house; but the green-haired man said he could not tarry, for he had many miles to sail that night.

'But when the sun comes up in the east,' added

the stranger, 'look for a thank-gift on the wild sea-shore.'

And behold, as morning dawned, the Viking saw a goodly vessel making gallant headway. As she drew near the land with streamer flying and broad sails flapping in the wind, the Viking saw that there was no soul on board of her, and yet without steersman to guide her the vessel avoided the shoals and held her way straight to the spot where he was standing.

Her prow was a dragon's head, a dragon's tail formed her stern, and dragon's wings bore her along swifter than an eagle before the storm.

The green-haired stranger was a sea-god, and the dragon-ship Ellide was his thank-gift.

Thus Frithiof, though only the son of a Thane, had treasures that might have been coveted by kings and princes. He sat in his father's halls, surrounded by his companions; upon his right was seated his bosom friend Bjorn, and twelve bold champions clad in steel were ranged around the board. And they drank in silence to the memory of Thorsten Vikingsson.

But suddenly the harps struck up, and the skalds

poured forth their songs in honour of the dead Thane.

And Frithiof's eyes filled with tears as he listened to his father's praises.

IV.

In spite of Frithiof's wealth, Helgi and Half-dan looked with disdain upon the son of their father's friend, and when Frithiof asked to have Ingebjorg for his wife, Helgi scornfully answered, ' My sister shall not wed the son of a Thane. If you like to be our serf, we will make room for you among our servants.'

Then went Frithiof away in wrath.

There was another suitor for the hand of Ingebjorg, good old King Ring, who, having lost his wife, thought that the Lily of the North would make a tender mother to his little son.

And he sent to Helgi and Halfdan to ask for Ingebjorg in marriage, but the brothers treated him as they had treated Frithiof ; and the old king was roused, and he swore he would revenge himself.

Helgi and Halfdan were afraid when they found that Ring was really making ready for war.   They began to get their army into order, and placed Ingebjorg for safety in the temple of Balder, and in their distress they even sent to Frithiof to ask him to come and help them.

They chose wisely in the messenger they sent to plead for them, for it was none other than old Hilding, who had been so kind to Frithiof in his childhood.

Frithiof was playing at chess with Bjorn when Hilding arrived. He pretended not to hear the message, and went on with his game.

'Shall the pawn save the king?' he asked of Bjorn.

And after a time he added,

'There is no other way to save the queen.' Which showed that he had been all the time occupied with Hilding's errand.

Therefore he returned with the old peasant, and contrived to see Ingebjorg in the temple of Balder and found that she still loved him as much as he loved her, and did not wish to marry anyone else.

And again he asked Helgi and Halfdan if they were willing that Ingebjorg should be his wife.

And again the brothers said Nay with scorn, and told him that he had profaned the temple of Balder by speaking to Ingebjorg within its walls.

O

'For such a misdeed,' said Helgi, 'death or banishment is the doom, and thou art in our power. Nevertheless, we are willing, as we wish to make thee useful to us, to forego the penalty. Thou shalt therefore sail forth to the distant Orkney Isles, and compel Jarl Angantyr to pay the tribute that he owes us.'

Frithiof would have refused to go, but Ingebjorg persuaded him to undertake the mission, for she was afraid of her brothers, and knew that Frithiof would be safer on the wild seas than in their hands.

At last Frithiof consented, and he took leave of Ingebjorg, and placed the golden bracelet that Völund had made upon her arm, praying her to keep it for his sake.

And then he sailed away over the heaving waters, and Ingebjorg mourned that her lover was gone.

V.

Over the sea. It was calm enough when Frithiof started; the storm-winds were asleep, and the waters heaved gently as though they would fain help speed the dragon-ship peacefully on her way.

But King Helgi standing on a rock repented that

he had suffered the noble Frithiof to escape his malice, and as he watched the good ship Ellide riding over the sea, he prayed loudly to the ocean fiends that they would trouble the waters and raise a fierce tempest to swallow up Frithiof and the dragon-ship.

All at once, the sparkling sea turned leaden grey, and the billows began to roll, the skies grew dark, and the howl of the driving wind was answered by a sullen roar from the depths beneath. Suddenly, a blinding flash of lightning played around the vessel, and as it vanished the pealing thunder burst from the clouds. The raging sea foamed, and seethed, and tossed the vessel like a feather upon its angry waves, and deeper sounded the thunder, and more fiercely flashed the lightning round the masts.

Wilder, wilder, wilder, grew the storm. Alas, for Frithiof!

'Ho! take the tiller in hand,' shouted Frithiof to Bjorn, 'and I will mount to the topmost mast and look out for danger.'

And when he looked out, he saw the storm-fiends riding on a whale. One was in form like to a great white bear, the other like unto a terrible eagle.

'Now help me, O gift of the sea-god! Help me, my gallant Ellide!' cried Frithiof.

And the dragon-ship heard her master's voice, and with her keel she smote the whale; so he died, and sank to the bottom of the sea, leaving the storm-fiends tossing upon the waves.

'Ho, spears and lances, help me in my need!' shouted Frithiof, as he took aim at the monsters.

And he transfixed the shrieking storm-fiends, and left them entangled in the huge coils of sea-weed which the storm had uprooted.

'Ho, ho!' laughed rugged Bjorn, 'they are trapped in their own nets.'

And so they were; and they were so much taken up with trying to free themselves from the seaweed and from Frithiof's long darts, that they were unable to give any heed to the storm, which therefore went down, and Frithiof and his crew sailed on, and reached the Orkney Isles in safety.

'Here comes Frithiof,' said the Viking Atlé. 'I know him by his dragon-ship.'

And forthwith the Viking rose and went forth; he had heard of the strength of Frithiof, and wished to match himself against him.

He did not wait to see whether Frithiof came in

enmity or friendship. Fighting was the first thing he thought of, and what he most cared for.

However, the Viking had the worst of it in the battle.

'There is witchcraft in thy sword,' said he to Frithiof.

So Frithiof threw his sword aside, and they wrestled together, unarmed, until Atlé was brought to the ground.

Then spake Frithiof: 'And if I had my sword thou wouldst not long be a living man.'

'Fetch it, then,' replied Atlé. 'I swear by the gods that I will not move until thou dost return.'

So Frithiof fetched his sword, but when he saw the conquered Viking still upon the ground, he could not bring himself to slay so honourable a man.

'Thou art too true and brave to die,' said Frithiof; 'rise, let us be friends.'

And the two combatants went hand in hand to the banquet hall of Angantyr, Jarl of the Orkney Islands.

A splendid hall it was, and a rare company of heroes was there, and all listened eagerly as Frithiof told his story, and wherefore he had come.

'I never paid tribute to King Belé, though he was an old friend of mine,' said the Jarl, as Frithiof ended his speech, 'nor will I to his sons. If they want aught of me let them come and take it.'

'It was by no choice of my own that I came upon such an errand,' returned Frithiof, 'and I shall be well content to carry back your answer.'

'Take also this purse of gold in token of friendship,' continued the Jarl, 'and remain with us, for I knew thy father.'

Thus Frithiof and the Jarl became good friends, and Frithiof consented to stay for awhile in the Orkney Islands; but after a time he ordered out his good ship Ellide, and set sail for his native land.

VI.

But fearful things had come to pass since he had left his home! Framnäs, the dwelling of his fathers, was a heap of ruins, and the land was waste and desolate.

And as he stood upon the well-loved spot, striving to find some traces of the past, his faithful hound bounded forth to greet him, and licked his master's hand. And then his favourite steed drew near, and thrust his nose into Frithiof's hand, hoping to find therein a piece of bread, as in the days of old. His favourite falcon perched upon his shoulder, and this was Frithiof's welcome to the home of his ancestors.

There had been a fierce battle, for King Ring with his army had come against Helgi and Halfdan, and the country had been laid waste, and many warriors slain.

And when all chance of withstanding him was at an end, the brothers, rather than lose their kingdom, had consented that Ingebjorg should be the wife of Ring.

Ingebjorg was married! Frithiof's heart was full of deep sorrow, and he turned his steps towards the temple of Balder, hoping that at the altar of the god he might meet with consolation.

In the temple he found King Helgi, and the sorrow that was weighing down Frithiof's heart gave place to hatred and revenge.

Caring nothing for the sacred place, he rushed madly forward. 'Here, take thy tribute,' said he, and he threw the purse that Jarl Angantyr had given him with such force against the face of the king that Helgi fell down senseless on the steps of the altar.

Next, seeing his arm-ring on the arm of the statue, for Helgi had taken it from Ingebjorg and placed it there, he tried to tear it off, and, lo ! the image tottered and fell upon the fire that was burning with sweet perfumes before it.

Scarcely had it touched the fire when it was ablaze, and the flames spreading rapidly on every side, the whole temple was soon a smouldering heap of ruins.

Then Frithiof sought his ship. He vowed that he would lead a Viking's life, and leave for ever a land where he had suffered so much sorrow. And he put out to sea.

But no sooner were his sails spread than he saw ten vessels in chase of him, and on the deck of one stood Helgi, who had been rescued from the burning temple, and had come in chase of him.

Yet Frithiof was rescued from the danger as if by miracle, for one by one the ships sank down as though some water giant had stretched out his strong arm, and dragged them below, and Helgi only saved himself by swimming ashore.

Loud laughed Bjorn.

'I bored holes in them last night,' said he, 'it is a rare ending to Helgi's fleet.'

'And now,' said Frithiof, 'I will for ever lead a Viking's life. I care not for aught upon the land. The sea shall be my home. And I will seek climes far away from here.'

So he steered the good ship Ellide southward, and among the isles of Greece strove to forget the memories of bygone days.

VII.

In and out of the sunny islands that lay like bosses of emerald on a silver shield sailed Frithiof, and on the deck of the dragon-ship he rested through the summer nights, looking up at the moon, and wondering what she could tell him of his northern land.

Sometimes he dreamed of his home as it was before the war-time. Sometimes he dreamed of the days when he and Ingebjorg roamed through the fields and woods together, or listened to old Hilding's stories by the blazing hearth, and then he would wake up with a start and stroke his faithful hound, who was ever near him, saying, 'Thou alone knowest no change ; to thee all is alike, so long as thy master is with thee.'

One night, however, as Frithiof was musing on the deck of his vessel, gazing into the cloudless sky, a vision of the past rose up before him; old familiar faces crowded round him, and in their midst he marked one, best beloved of all, pale, sad with sorrowful eyes, and her lips moved, and he seemed to hear her say, ' I am very sad without thee, Frithiof.'

Then a great longing came upon Frithiof to see Ingebjorg once more. He would go northward, even to the country of King Ring; he must see Ingebjorg. What did he care for danger ? He must go.

To the cold dark north.

Yet he dared not go openly, for King Ring looked upon him as an enemy, and would seize him at once, and if he did not kill him would shut him up in prison, so that either way he would not see the beautiful queen.

Frithiof therefore disguised himself as an old man, and, wrapped in bearskins, presented himself at the palace.

The old king sat upon his throne, and at his side

was Ingebjorg the Fair, looking like spring by the side of fading autumn.

As the strangely dressed figure passed along, the courtiers jeered, and Frithiof, thrown off his guard, angrily seized one of them, and twirled him round with but little effort.

'Ho!' said the king, 'thou art a strong old man, O stranger! Whence art thou?'

'I was reared in anguish and want,' returned Frithiof; 'sorrow has filled a bitter cup for me, and I have almost drunk it to the dregs. Once I rode upon a dragon, but now it lies dead upon the sea-shore, and I am left in my old age to burn salt upon the strand.'

'Thou art not old,' answered the wise king; 'thy voice is clear, and thy grasp strong. Throw off thy rude disguise, that we may know our guest.'

Then Frithiof threw aside his bearskin, and appeared clad in a mantle of blue embroidered velvet, and his hair fell like a golden wave upon his shoulder.

Ring did not know him, but Ingebjorg did; and when she handed the goblet for him to drink, her colour went and came 'like to the northern light on a field of snow.'

And Frithiof stayed at the court until the year came round again, and spring once more put forth its early blossoms.

One day a gay hunting train went forth, but old King Ring, not being strong, as in former years, lay down to rest upon the mossy turf beneath some arching pines, whilst the hunters rode on.

Then Frithiof drew near, and in his heart wild thoughts arose. One blow of his sword, and Ingebjorg was free to be his wife.

But as he looked upon the sleeping king, there came a whisper from a better voice, ' It is cowardly to strike a sleeping foe.'

And Frithiof shuddered, for he was too brave a man to commit murder.

' Sleep on, old man,' he muttered gently to himself.

But Ring's sleep was over.   He started up.   ' O Frithiof, why hast thou come hither to steal an old man's bride ?'

' I came not hither for so dark a purpose,' answered Frithiof; ' I came but to look on the face of my loved Ingebjorg once more.'

' I know it,' replied the King, ' I have tried thee, I have proved thee, and true as tried steel hast thou passed through the furnace. Stay with us yet a little longer, the old man soon will be gathered to his fathers, then shall his kingdom and his wife be thine.'

But Frithiof replied that he had already remained too long, and that on the morrow he must depart.

Yet he went not, for death had visited the palace, and old King Ring was stretched upon his bier, whilst the bards around sang of his wisdom.

Then arose a cry among the people, 'We must choose a king!'

And Frithiof raised aloft upon his shield the little son of Ring.

'Here is your king,' he said, 'the son of wise old Ring.'

The blue-eyed child laughed and clapped his hands as he beheld the glittering helmets and glancing spears of the warriors. Then tired of his high place, he sprang down into the midst of them.

Loud uprose the shout, 'The child shall be our king, and the Jarl Frithiof regent. Hail to the young king of the Northmen!'

VIII.

But Frithiof in the hour of his good fortune did not forget that he had offended the gods. He must make atonement to Balder for having caused the ruin of his temple. He must turn his steps once more homeward.

Home! Home! And on his father's grave he sank down with a softened heart, and grieved over the passion and revenge that had swayed his deeds. And as he mourned, the voices of unseen spirits answered him, and whispered that he was forgiven.

And to his wondering eyes a vision was vouch-safed, and the temple of Balder appeared before him, rebuilt in more than its ancient splendour, and deep peace sank into the soul of Frithiof.

'Rise up, rise up, Frithiof, and journey onward.'

The words came clear as a command to Frithiof, and he obeyed them. He rose up, and journeyed to the place where he had left the temple a heap of blackened ruins.

And, lo! the vision that had appeared to him was accomplished, for there stood the beautiful building, stately and fair to look upon. So beauti-ful, that, as he gazed, his thoughts were of Valhalla.

He entered, and the white-robed silver-bearded priest welcomed the long absent Viking, and told him that Helgi was dead, and Halfdan reigned alone.

' And know, O Frithiof,' said the aged man, 'that Balder is better pleased when the heart grows soft and injuries are forgiven, than with the most costly sacrifices. Lay aside for ever all thoughts of hatred and revenge, and stretch out to Halfdan the hand of friendship.'

Joy had softened all Frithiof's feelings of anger, and, advancing to Halfdan, who was standing near the altar, he spoke out manfully.

' Halfdan,' he said, ' let us forget the years that have gone by. Let all past evil and injury be buried in the grave. Henceforth let us be as brothers, and once more I ask thee, give me Ingebjorg to be my wife.'

And Halfdan made answer, ' Thou shalt be my brother.'

And as he spoke, an inner door flew open, and a sweet chorus of youthful voices was heard. A band of maidens issued forth, and at their head walked Ingebjorg fairer than ever.

Then Halfdan, leading her to Frithiof, placed her hand within that of the Viking.

'Behold thy wife,' said Halfdan. 'Well hast thou won her. May the gods attend upon your bridal.'

So Ingebjorg became the wife of Frithiof at last.

Thus steps of sorrow had but led them to a height of happiness that poets love to sing. Paths thick with thorns had blossomed into roses, and wreaths of everlasting flowers had crowned the winter snows. And midst the lights and shadows of the old North land, their lives flowed on like to two united streams that roll through quiet pastures to the ocean of eternity.

LONDON: PRINTED BY
SPOTTISWOODE AND CO., NEW-STREET SQUARE
AND PARLIAMENT STREET

[SEPTEMBER 1870.]

GENERAL LIST OF WORKS

PUBLISHED BY

MESSRS. LONGMANS, GREEN, AND CO.

PATERNOSTER ROW, LONDON.

History, Politics, Historical Memoirs, &c.

The **HISTORY of ENGLAND** from the Fall of Wolsey to the Defeat of the Spanish Armada. By JAMES ANTHONY FROUDE, M.A. late Fellow of Exeter College, Oxford.
> LIBRARY EDITION, 12 VOLS. 8vo. price £8 18s.
> CABINET EDITION, now appearing, in 12 vols. crown 8vo. price 6s. each.

The **HISTORY of ENGLAND** from the Accession of James II. By Lord MACAULAY.
> LIBRARY EDITION, 5 vols. 8vo. £4.
> CABINET EDITION, 8 vols. post 8vo. 48s.
> PEOPLE'S EDITION, 4 vols. crown 8vo. 16s.

LORD MACAULAY'S WORKS. Complete and Uniform Library Edition. Edited by his Sister, Lady TREVELYAN. 8 vols. 8vo. with Portrait, price £5 5s. cloth, or £8 8s. bound in tree-calf by Rivière.

An **ESSAY** on the **HISTORY of the ENGLISH GOVERNMENT** and Constitution, from the Reign of Henry VII. to the Present Time. By JOHN EARL RUSSELL. Fourth Edition, revised. Crown 8vo. 6s.

SELECTIONS from SPEECHES of EARL RUSSELL, 1817 to 1841, and from Despatches, 1859 to 1865; with Introductions. 2 vols. 8vo. 28s.

VARIETIES of VICE-REGAL LIFE. By Sir WILLIAM DENISON, K.C.B. late Governor-General of the Australian Colonies, and Governor of Madras. With Two Maps. 2 vols. 8vo. 28s.

On **PARLIAMENTARY GOVERNMENT** in **ENGLAND**: Its Origin, Development, and Practical Operation. By ALPHEUS TODD, Librarian of the Legislative Assembly of Canada. 2 vols. 8vo. price £1 17s.

LAND SYSTEMS and INDUSTRIAL ECONOMY of IRELAND, ENGLAND, and CONTINENTAL COUNTRIES. By T. E. CLIFFE LESLIE, LL.B. of Lincoln's Inn, Barrister-at-Law. 8vo. 12s.

A **HISTORICAL ACCOUNT of the NEUTRALITY of GREAT BRITAIN DURING the AMERICAN CIVIL WAR.** By MOUNTAGUE BERNARD, M.A. Chichele Professor of International Law and Diplomacy in the University of Oxford. Royal 8vo. 16s.

A

The HISTORY of ENGLAND during the Reign of George the Third. By the Right Hon. W. N. MASSEY. Cabinet Edition. 4 vols. post 8vo. 24s.

The CONSTITUTIONAL HISTORY of ENGLAND, since the Accession of George III. 1760—1860. By Sir THOMAS ERSKINE MAY, C.B. Second Edition. 2 vols. 8vo. 33s.

HISTORICAL STUDIES. By HERMAN MERIVALE, M.A.   8vo. 12s. 6d.

The OXFORD REFORMERS of 1498—John Colet, Erasmus, and Thomas More; being a History of their Fellow-work. By FREDERIC SEEBOHM. Second Edition, enlarged. 8vo. 14s.

A HISTORY of WALES, derived from Authentic Sources. By JANE WILLIAMS, Ysgafell. 8vo. 14s.

LECTURES on the HISTORY of ENGLAND, from the earliest Times to the Death of King Edward II. By WILLIAM LONGMAN. With Maps and Illustrations. 8vo. 15s.

The HISTORY of the LIFE and TIMES of EDWARD the THIRD. By WILLIAM LONGMAN. With 9 Maps, 8 Plates, and 16 Woodcuts. 2 vols. 8vo. 28s.

HISTORY of the NORMAN KINGS of ENGLAND, from a New Collation of the Contemporary Chronicles. By THOMAS COBBE, Barrister, of the Inner Temple. 8vo. price 16s.

The OVERTHROW of the GERMANIC CONFEDERATION by PRUSSIA in 1866. By Sir ALEXANDER MALET, Bart. K.C.B. With 5 Maps. 8vo. 18s.

The MILITARY RESOURCES of PRUSSIA and FRANCE, and RECENT CHANGES in the ART of WAR. By Lieut.-Col. CHESNEY, R.E. and HENRY REEVE, D.C.L. Crown 8vo. price 7s. 6d.

WATERLOO LECTURES: a Study of the Campaign of 1815. By Colonel CHARLES C. CHESNEY, R.E. late Professor of Military Art and History in the Staff College. New Edition. 8vo. with Map, 10s. 6d.

DEMOCRACY in AMERICA. By ALEXIS DE TOCQUEVILLE. Translated by HENRY REEVE. 2 vols. 8vo. 21s.

HISTORY of the REFORMATION in EUROPE in the Time of Calvin. By J. H. MERLE D'AUBIGNÉ, D.D. VOLS. I. and II. 8vo. 28s. VOL. III. 12s. VOL. IV. 16s. VOL. V. price 16s.

HISTORY of FRANCE, from Clovis and Charlemagne to the Accession of Napoléon III. By EYRE EVANS CROWE. 5 vols. 8vo. £4 13s.

CHAPTERS from FRENCH HISTORY; St. Louis, Joan of Arc, Henri IV. with Sketches of the Intermediate Periods. By J. H. GURNEY, M.A. New Edition. Fcp. 8vo. 6s. 6d.

MEMOIR of POPE SIXTUS the FIFTH. By Baron HUBNER. Translated from the Original in French, with the Author's sanction, by HUBERT E. H. JERNINGHAM. 2 vols. 8vo.   [Nearly ready.

IGNATIUS LOYOLA and the EARLY JESUITS. By STEWART ROSE. 8vo. with Portrait, price 16s.

The HISTORY of GREECE. By C. THIRLWALL, D.D. Lord Bishop of St. David's. 8 vols. fcp. 8vo. price 28s.

GREEK HISTORY from Themistocles to Alexander, in a Series of Lives from Plutarch. Revised and arranged by A. H. CLOUGH. Fcp. with 44 Woodcuts, 6s.

CRITICAL HISTORY of the **LANGUAGE** and **LITERATURE** of Ancient Greece. By WILLIAM MURE, of Caldwell. 5 vols. 8vo. £3 9s.

The TALE of the GREAT PERSIAN WAR, from the Histories of Herodotus. By GEORGE W. COX, M.A. New Edition. Fcp. 3s. 6d.

HISTORY of the LITERATURE of ANCIENT GREECE. By Professor K. O. MÜLLER. Translated by the Right Hon. Sir GEORGE CORNEWALL LEWIS, Bart. and by J. W. DONALDSON, D.D. 3 vols. 8vo. 21s.

HISTORY of the CITY of ROME from its Foundation to the Sixteenth Century of the Christian Era. By THOMAS H. DYER, LL.D. 8vo. with 2 Maps, 15s.

The HISTORY of ROME. By WILHELM IHNE. Translated and revised by the Author. VOLS. I. and II. 8vo. [Nearly ready.

HISTORY of the ROMANS under the **EMPIRE.** By the Very Rev. C. MERIVALE, D.C.L. Dean of Ely. 8 vols. post 8vo. 48s.

The FALL of the ROMAN REPUBLIC; a Short History of the Last Century of the Commonwealth. By the same Author. 12mo. 7s. 6d.

The STUDENT'S MANUAL of the HISTORY of INDIA, from the Earliest Period to the Present. By Colonel MEADOWS TAYLOR, M.R.A.S. M.R.I.A. Author of 'The Confessions of a Thug.' Crown 8vo. [In the press.

The HISTORY of INDIA, from the Earliest Period to the close of Lord Dalhousie's Administration. By JOHN CLARK MARSHMAN. 3 vols. crown 8vo. 22s. 6d.

INDIAN POLITY: a View of the System of Administration in India. By Lieutenant-Colonel GEORGE CHESNEY, Fellow of the University of Calcutta. New Edition, revised; with Map. 8vo. price 21s.

HOME POLITICS; being a consideration of the Causes of the Growth of Trade in relation to Labour, Pauperism, and Emigration. By DANIEL GRANT. 8vo. 7s.

REALITIES of IRISH LIFE. By W. STEUART TRENCH, Land Agent in Ireland to the Marquess of Lansdowne, the Marquess of Bath, and Lord Digby. Fifth Edition. Crown 8vo. price 6s.

The STUDENT'S MANUAL of the HISTORY of IRELAND. By MARY F. CUSACK, Authoress of the 'Illustrated of Ireland, from the Earliest Period to the Year of Catholic Emancipation.' Crown 8vo. price 6s.

CRITICAL and HISTORICAL ESSAYS contributed to the *Edinburgh Review*. By the Right Hon. LORD MACAULAY.
CABINET EDITION, 4 vols. post 8vo. 24s. LIBRARY EDITION, 3 vols. 8vo. 36s.
PEOPLE'S EDITION, 2 vols. crown 8vo. 8s. STUDENT'S EDITION, 1 vol. cr. 8vo. 6s.

HISTORY of EUROPEAN MORALS, from Augustus to Charlemagne. By W. E. H. LECKY, M.A. Second Edition. 2 vols. 8vo. price 28s.

HISTORY of the RISE and INFLUENCE of the SPIRIT of RATIONALISM in EUROPE. By W. E. H. LECKY, M.A. Cabinet Edition, being the Fourth. 2 vols. crown 8vo. price 16s.

GOD in HISTORY; or, the Progress of Man's Faith in the Moral Order of the World. By Baron BUNSEN. Translated by SUSANNA WINKWORTH; with a Preface by Dean STANLEY. 3 vols. 8vo. price 42s.

Criticism, Philosophy, Polity, &c.

The **INSTITUTES of JUSTINIAN**; with English Introduction, Translation, and Notes. By T. C. SANDARS, M.A. Barrister, late Fellow of Oriel Coll. Oxon. New Edition. 8vo. 15s.

SOCRATES and the **SOCRATIC SCHOOLS.** Translated from the German of Dr. E. ZELLER, with the Author's approval, by the Rev. OSWALD J. REICHEL, B.C.L. and M.A. Crown 8vo. 8s. 6d.

The **STOICS, EPICUREANS,** and **SCEPTICS.** Translated from the German of Dr. E. ZELLER, with the Author's approval, by OSWALD J. REICHEL, B.C.L. and M.A. Crown 8vo. price 14s.

The **ETHICS of ARISTOTLE,** illustrated with Essays and Notes. By Sir A. GRANT, Bart. M.A. LL.D. Second Edition, revised and completed. 2 vols. 8vo. price 28s.

The **NICOMACHEAN ETHICS of ARISTOTLE** newly translated into English. By R. WILLIAMS, B.A. Fellow and late Lecturer of Merton College, and sometime Student of Christ Church, Oxford. 8vo. 12s.

ELEMENTS of LOGIC. By R. WHATELY, D.D. late Archbishop of Dublin. New Edition. 8vo. 10s. 6d. crown 8vo. 4s. 6d.

Elements of Rhetoric. By the same Author. New Edition. 8vo. 10s. 6d. crown 8vo. 4s. 6d.

English Synonymes. By E. JANE WHATELY. Edited by Archbishop WHATELY. 5th Edition. Fcp. 3s.

BACON'S ESSAYS with ANNOTATIONS. By R. WHATELY, D.D. late Archbishop of Dublin. Sixth Edition. 8vo. 10s. 6d.

LORD BACON'S WORKS, collected and edited by J. SPEDDING, M.A. R. L. ELLIS, M.A. and D. D. HEATH. New and Cheaper Edition. 7 vols. 8vo. price £3 13s. 6d.

ENGLAND and IRELAND. By JOHN STUART MILL. Fifth Edition, vo. 1s.

The **SUBJECTION of WOMEN.** By JOHN STUART MILL. New Edition. Post 8vo. 5s.

On **REPRESENTATIVE GOVERNMENT.** By JOHN STUART MILL. Third Edition. 8vo. 9s. Crown 8vo. 2s.

On **LIBERTY.** By JOHN STUART MILL. Fourth Edition. Post 8vo. 7s. 6d. Crown 8vo. 1s. 4d.

Principles of Political Economy. By the same Author. Sixth Edition. 2 vols. 8vo. 30s. Or in 1 vol. crown 8vo. 5s.

A System of Logic, Ratiocinative and Inductive. By the same Author. Seventh Edition. Two vols. 8vo. 25s.

ANALYSIS of Mr. MILL'S SYSTEM of LOGIC. By W. STEBBING, M.A. Fellow of Worcester College, Oxford. New Edition. 12mo. 3s. 6d.

UTILITARIANISM. By JOHN STUART MILL. Third Edition. 8vo. 5s.

DISSERTATIONS and **DISCUSSIONS, POLITICAL, PHILOSOPHI-CAL,** and **HISTORICAL.** By JOHN STUART MILL. Second Edition, revised. 3 vols. 8vo. 36s.

EXAMINATION of Sir W. HAMILTON'S PHILOSOPHY, and of the Principal Philosophical Questions discussed in his Writings. By JOHN STUART MILL. Third Edition. 8vo. 16s.

An **OUTLINE of the NECESSARY LAWS of THOUGHT:** a Treatise on Pure and Applied Logic. By the Most Rev. WILLIAM, Lord Archbishop of York, D.D. F.R.S. Ninth Thousand. Crown 8vo. 5s. 6d.

The **ELEMENTS of POLITICAL ECONOMY.** By HENRY DUNNING MACLEOD, M.A. Barrister-at-Law. 8vo. 16s.

A **Dictionary of Political Economy;** Biographical, Bibliographical, Historical, and Practical. By the same Author. VOL. I. royal 8vo. 30s.

The **ELECTION of REPRESENTATIVES,** Parliamentary and Municipal; a Treatise. By THOMAS HARE, Barrister-at-Law. Third Edition, with Additions. Crown 8vo. 6s.

SPEECHES of the RIGHT HON. LORD MACAULAY, corrected by Himself. People's Edition, crown 8vo. 3s. 6d.

Lord Macaulay's Speeches on Parliamentary Reform in 1831 and 1832. 16mo. 1s.

INAUGURAL ADDRESS delivered to the University of St. Andrews. By JOHN STUART MILL. 8vo. 5s. People's Edition, crown 8vo. 1s.

A **DICTIONARY of the ENGLISH LANGUAGE.** By R. G. LATHAM, M.A. M.D. F.R.S. Founded on the Dictionary of Dr. SAMUEL JOHNSON, as edited by the Rev. H. J. TODD, with numerous Emendations and Additions. In Four Volumes, 4to. price £7.

THESAURUS of ENGLISH WORDS and PHRASES, classified and arranged so as to facilitate the Expression of Ideas, and assist in Literary Composition. By P. M. ROGET, M.D. New Edition. Crown 8vo. 10s. 6d.

LECTURES on the SCIENCE of LANGUAGE, delivered at the Royal Institution. By MAX MÜLLER, M.A. Fellow of All Souls College, Oxford. 2 vols. 8vo. price 30s.

CHAPTERS on LANGUAGE. By FREDERIC W. FARRAR, F.R.S. late Fellow of Trin. Coll. Cambridge. Crown 8vo. 8s. 6d.

WORD-GOSSIP; a Series of Familiar Essays on Words and their Peculiarities. By the Rev. W. L. BLACKLEY, M.A. Fcp. 8vo. 5s.

A **BOOK ABOUT WORDS.** By G. F. GRAHAM, Author of 'English, or the Art of Composition,' &c. Fcp. 8vo. price 3s. 6d.

The **DEBATER;** a Series of Complete Debates, Outlines of Debates, and Questions for Discussion. By F. ROWTON. Fcp. 6s.

MANUAL of ENGLISH LITERATURE, Historical and Critical. By THOMAS ARNOLD, M.A. Second Edition. Crown 8vo. price 7s. 6d.

SOUTHEY'S DOCTOR, complete in One Volume. Edited by the Rev. J. W. WARTER, B.D. Square crown 8vo. 12s. 6d.

HISTORICAL and CRITICAL COMMENTARY on the OLD TESTA-MENT; with a New Translation. By M. M. KALISCH, Ph.D. VOL. I. *Genesis,* 8vo. 18s. or adapted for the General Reader, 12s. VOL. II. *Exodus,* 15s. or adapted for the General Reader, 12s. VOL. III. *Leviticus,* PART I. 15s. or adapted for the General Reader, 8s.

A HEBREW GRAMMAR, with EXERCISES. By M. M. KALISCH, Ph.D. PART I. *Outlines with Exercises*, 8vo. 12s. 6d. KEY, 5s. PART II. *Exceptional Forms and Constructions*, 12s. 6d.

A LATIN-ENGLISH DICTIONARY. By J. T. WHITE, D.D. of Corpus Christi College, and J. E. RIDDLE, M.A. of St. Edmund Hall, Oxford. Third Edition, revised. 2 vols. 4to. pp. 2,128, price 42s. cloth.

White's College Latin-English Dictionary (Intermediate Size), abridged for the use of University Students from the Parent Work (as above). Medium 8vo. pp. 1,048, price 18s. cloth.

White's Junior Student's Complete Latin-English and English-Latin Dictionary. New Edition. Square 12mo. pp. 1,058, price 12s.

Separately { The ENGLISH-LATIN DICTIONARY, price 5s. 6d.
              { The LATIN-ENGLISH DICTIONARY, price 7s. 6d.

An ENGLISH-GREEK LEXICON, containing all the Greek Words used by Writers of good authority. By C. D. YONGE, B.A. New Edition. 4to. 21s.

Mr. YONGE'S NEW LEXICON, English and Greek, abridged from his larger work (as above): Revised Edition. Square 12mo. 8s. 6d.

A GREEK-ENGLISH LEXICON. Compiled by H. G. LIDDELL, D.D. Dean of Christ Church, and R. SCOTT, D.D. Master of Balliol. Sixth Edition. Crown 4to. price 36s.

A Lexicon, Greek and English, abridged from LIDDELL and SCOTT's *Greek-English Lexicon.* Twelfth Edition. Square 12mo. 7s. 6d.

A SANSKRIT-ENGLISH DICTIONARY, the Sanskrit words printed both in the original Devanagari and in Roman Letters. Compiled by T. BENFEY, Prof. in the Univ. of Göttingen. 8vo. 52s. 6d.

WALKER'S PRONOUNCING DICTIONARY of the ENGLISH LAN- GUAGE. Thoroughly revised Editions, by B. H. SMART. 8vo. 12s. 16mo. 6s.

A PRACTICAL DICTIONARY of the FRENCH and ENGLISH LAN- GUAGES. By L. CONTANSEAU. Fourteenth Edition. Post 8vo. 10s. 6d.

Contanseau's Pocket Dictionary, French and English, abridged from the above by the Author. New Edition, revised. Square 18mo. 3s. 6d.

NEW PRACTICAL DICTIONARY of the GERMAN LANGUAGE; German–English and English-German. By the Rev. W. L. BLACKLEY, M.A. and Dr. CARL MARTIN FRIEDLÄNDER. Post 8vo. 7s. 6d.

The MASTERY of LANGUAGES; or, the Art of Speaking Foreign Tongues Idiomatically. By THOMAS PRENDERGAST, late of the Civil Service at Madras. Second Edition. 8vo. 6s.

Miscellaneous Works and *Popular Metaphysics.*

The ESSAYS and CONTRIBUTIONS of A. K. H. B., Author of 'The Recreations of a Country Parson.' Uniform Editions:—

Recreations of a Country Parson. By A. K. H. B. FIRST and SECOND SERIES. crown 8vo. 3s. 6d. each.

The Common-place Philosopher in Town and Country. By A. K. H. B. Crown 8vo. price 3s. 6d.

Leisure Hours in Town; Essays Consolatory, Æsthetical, Moral, Social, and Domestic. By A. K. H. B. Crown 8vo. 3s. 6d.

The Autumn Holidays of a Country Parson; Essays contributed to *Fraser's Magazine* and to *Good Words*. By A. K. H. B. Crown 8vo. 3s. 6d.

The Graver Thoughts of a Country Parson. By A. K. H. B. FIRST and SECOND SERIES, crown 8vo. 3s. 6d. each.

Critical Essays of a Country Parson, selected from Essays contributed to *Fraser's Magazine*. By A. K. H. B. Crown 8vo. 3s. 6d.

Sunday Afternoons at the Parish Church of a Scottish University City. By A. K. H. B. Crown 8vo. 3s. 6d.

Lessons of Middle Age; with some Account of various Cities and Men. By A. K. H. B. Crown 8vo. 3s. 6d.

Counsel and Comfort spoken from a City Pulpit. By A. K. H. B. Crown 8vo. price 3s. 6d.

Changed Aspects of Unchanged Truths; Memorials of St. Andrews Sundays. By A. K. H. B. Crown 8vo. 3s. 6d.

SHORT STUDIES on GREAT SUBJECTS. By JAMES ANTHONY FROUDE, M.A. late Fellow of Exeter Coll. Oxford. Third Edition. 8vo. 12s.

LORD MACAULAY'S MISCELLANEOUS WRITINGS :—
LIBRARY EDITION. 2 vols. 8vo. Portrait, 21s.
PEOPLE'S EDITION. 1 vol. crown 8vo. 4s. 6d.

The REV. SYDNEY SMITH'S MISCELLANEOUS WORKS; including his Contributions to the *Edinburgh Review*. Crown 8vo. 6s.

The Wit and Wisdom of the Rev. Sydney Smith: a Selection of the most memorable Passages in his Writings and Conversation. 16mo. 3s. 6d.

TRACES of HISTORY in the NAMES of PLACES; with a Vocabulary of the Roots out of which Names of Places in England and Wales are formed. By FLAVELL EDMUNDS. Crown 8vo. 7s. 6d.

ESSAYS selected from CONTRIBUTIONS to the *Edinburgh Review*. By HENRY ROGERS. Second Edition. 3 vols. fcp. 21s.

Reason and Faith, their Claims and Conflicts. By the same Author. New Edition, accompanied by several other Essays. Crown 8vo. 6s. 6d.

The Eclipse of Faith; or, a Visit to a Religious Sceptic. By the same Author. Twelfth Edition. Fcp. 5s.

Defence of the Eclipse of Faith, by its Author; a rejoinder to Dr. Newman's *Reply*. Third Edition. Fcp. 3s. 6d.

Selections from the Correspondence of R. E. H. Greyson. By the same Author. Third Edition. Crown 8vo. 7s. 6d.

FAMILIES of SPEECH, Four Lectures delivered at the Royal Institution of Great Britain. By the Rev. F. W. FARRAR, M.A. F.R.S. late Fellow of Trinity College, Cambridge. Post 8vo. with Two Maps, 5s. 6d.

B

CHIPS from a **GERMAN WORKSHOP**; being Essays on the Science of Religion, and on Mythology, Traditions, and Customs. By MAX MÜLLER, M.A. Fellow of All Souls College, Oxford. Second Edition, revised, with an Index. 2 vols. 8vo. 24s.

ANALYSIS of the PHENOMENA of the **HUMAN MIND.** By JAMES MILL. A New Edition, with Notes, Illustrative and Critical, by ALEXANDER BAIN, ANDREW FINDLATER, and GEORGE GROTE. Edited, with additional Notes, by JOHN STUART MILL. 2 vols. 8vo. price 28s.

An **INTRODUCTION** to **MENTAL PHILOSOPHY,** on the Inductive Method. By J. D. MORELL, M.A. LL.D. 8vo. 12s.

ELEMENTS of **PSYCHOLOGY,** containing the Analysis of the Intellectual Powers. By the same Author. Post 8vo. 7s. 6d.

The SECRET of **HEGEL**: being the Hegelian System in Origin, Principle, Form, and Matter. By J. H. STIRLING. 2 vols. 8vo. 28s.

The SENSES and the **INTELLECT.** By ALEXANDER BAIN, M.D. Professor of Logic in the University of Aberdeen. Third Edition. 8vo. 15s.

The EMOTIONS and the **WILL.** By the same Author. Second Edition. 8vo. 15s.

On the **STUDY of CHARACTER,** including an Estimate of Phrenology. By the same Author. 8vo. 9s.

MENTAL and **MORAL SCIENCE**: a Compendium of Psychology and Ethics. By the same Author. Second Edition. Crown 8vo. 10s. 6d.

LOGIC, **DEDUCTIVE** and **INDUCTIVE.** By the same Author. In TWO PARTS, crown 8vo. 10s. 6d. Each Part may be had separately:—
PART I. *Deduction,* 4s. PART II. *Induction,* 6s. 6d.

TIME and **SPACE;** a Metaphysical Essay. By SHADWORTH H. HODGSON. (This work covers the whole ground of Speculative Philosophy.) 8vo. price 16s.

The Theory of **Practice;** an Ethical Inquiry. By the same Author. (This work, in conjunction with the foregoing, completes a system of Philosophy.) 2 vols. 8vo. price 24s.

STRONG AND **FREE;** or, First Steps towards Social Science. By the Author of 'My Life, and What shall I do with it?' 8vo. price 10s. 6d.

The PHILOSOPHY of **NECESSITY;** or, Natural Law as applicable to Mental, Moral, and Social Science. By CHARLES BRAY. Second Edition. 8vo. 9s.

The Education of the **Feelings** and **Affections.** By the same Author. Third Edition. 8vo. 3s. 6d.

On Force, its **Mental** and **Moral Correlates.** By the same Author. 8vo. 5s.

CHARACTERISTICS of **MEN, MANNERS, OPINIONS, TIMES.** By ANTHONY, Third Earl of SHAFTESBURY. Published from the Edition of 1713, with Engravings designed by the Author; and edited, with Marginal Analysis, Notes, and Illustrations, by the Rev. W. M. HATCH, M.A. Fellow of New College, Oxford. 3 vols. 8vo. VOL. I. price 14s.

A TREATISE on **HUMAN NATURE**; being an Attempt to Introduce the Experimental Method of Reasoning into Moral Subjects. By DAVID HUME. Edited, with a Preliminary Dissertation and Notes, by T. H. GREEN, Fellow, and T. H. GROSE, late Scholar, of Balliol College, Oxford.
[In the press.

ESSAYS MORAL, **POLITICAL,** and **LITERARY.** By DAVID HUME. By the same Editors.
[In the press.

Astronomy, Meteorology, Popular Geography, &c.

OUTLINES of ASTRONOMY. By Sir J. F. W. HERSCHEL, Bart.
M.A. Tenth Edition, revised; with 9 Plates and many Woodcuts. 8vo. 18s.

OTHER WORLDS THAN OURS; the Plurality of Worlds Studied
under the Light of Recent Scientific Researches. By RICHARD A. PROCTOR,
B.A. F.R.A.S. With 13 Illustrations (6 of them coloured). Crown 8vo. 10s. 6d.

SATURN and its SYSTEM. By the same Author. 8vo. with 14 Plates, 14s.

CELESTIAL OBJECTS for COMMON TELESCOPES. By the Rev.
T. W. WEBB, M.A. F.R.A.S. Second Edition, revised, with a large Map of
the Moon, and several Woodcuts. 16mo. 7s. 6d.

NAVIGATION and NAUTICAL ASTRONOMY (Practical, Theoretical,
Scientific) for the use of Students and Practical Men. By J. MERRIFIELD,
F.R.A.S and H. EVERS. 8vo. 14s.

DOVE'S LAW of STORMS, considered in connexion with the Ordinary
Movements of the Atmosphere. Translated by R. H. SCOTT, M.A. T.C.D.
8vo. 10s. 6d.

PHYSICAL GEOGRAPHY for SCHOOLS and GENERAL READERS.
By M. F. MAURY, LL.D. Fcp. with 2 Charts, 2s. 6d.

M'CULLOCH'S DICTIONARY, Geographical, Statistical, and Historical,
of the various Countries, Places, and Principal Natural Objects in the World.
New Edition, with the Statistical Information brought up to the latest
returns by F. MARTIN. 4 vols. 8vo. with coloured Maps, £4 4s.

A GENERAL DICTIONARY of GEOGRAPHY, Descriptive, Physical,
Statistical, and Historical: forming a complete Gazetteer of the World. By
A. KEITH JOHNSTON, LL.D. F.R.G.S. Revised Edition. 8vo. 31s. 6d.

A MANUAL of GEOGRAPHY, Physical, Industrial, and Political.
By W. HUGHES, F.R.G.S. With 6 Maps. Fcp. 7s. 6d.

The STATES of the RIVER PLATE: their Industries and Commerce.
By WILFRID LATHAM, Buenos Ayres. Second Edition, revised. 8vo. 12s.

MAUNDER'S TREASURY of GEOGRAPHY, Physical, Historical,
Descriptive, and Political. Edited by W. HUGHES, F.R.G.S. Revised
Edition, with 7 Maps and 16 Plates. Fcp. 6s. cloth, or 9s. 6d. bound in calf.

Natural History and *Popular Science.*

ELEMENTARY TREATISE on PHYSICS, Experimental and Applied.
Translated and edited from GANOT'S *Eléments de Physique* (with the Author's sanction) by E. ATKINSON, Ph.D. F.C.S. New Edition, revised
and enlarged; with a Coloured Plate and 620 Woodcuts. Post 8vo. 15s.

The ELEMENTS of PHYSICS or NATURAL PHILOSOPHY. By
NEIL ARNOTT, M.D. F.R.S. Physician Extraordinary to the Queen. Sixth
Edition, rewritten and completed. Two Parts, 8vo. 21s.

SOUND: a Course of Eight Lectures delivered at the Royal Institution
of Great Britain. By JOHN TYNDALL, LL.D. F.R.S. New Edition, crown
8vo. with Portrait of *M. Chladni* and 169 Woodcuts, price 9s.

HEAT a MODE of MOTION. By Professor JOHN TYNDALL, LL.D.
F.R.S. Fourth Edition. Crown 8vo. with Woodcuts, 10*s.* 6*d.*

**RESEARCHES on DIAMAGNETISM and MAGNE-CRYSTALLIC
ACTION**; including the Question of Diamagnetic Polarity. By the same
Author. With 6 Plates and many Woodcuts. 8vo. price 14*s.*

NOTES of a COURSE of NINE LECTURES on LIGHT delivered at the
Royal Institution of Great Britain in April–June 1869. By the same Author.
Crown 8vo. price 1*s.* sewed, or 1*s.* 6*d.* cloth.

LIGHT: Its Influence on Life and Health. By FORBES WINSLOW,
M.D. D.C.L. Oxon. (Hon.). Fcp. 8vo. 6*s.*

A TREATISE on ELECTRICITY, in Theory and Practice. By A.
DE LA RIVE, Prof. in the Academy of Geneva. Translated by C. V. WALKER,
F.R.S. 3 vols. 8vo. with Woodcuts, £3 13*s.*

The CORRELATION of PHYSICAL FORCES. By W. R. GROVE,
Q.C. V.P.R.S. Fifth Edition, revised, and followed by a Discourse on Continuity. 8vo. 10*s.* 6*d.* The *Discourse on Continuity*, separately, 2*s.* 6*d.*

MANUAL of GEOLOGY. By S. HAUGHTON, M.D. F.R.S. Revised
Edition, with 66 Woodcuts. Fcp. 7*s.* 6*d.*

A GUIDE to GEOLOGY. By J. PHILLIPS, M.A. Professor of Geology
in the University of Oxford. Fifth Edition, with Plates. Fcp. 4*s.*

**The STUDENT'S MANUAL of ZOOLOGY and COMPARATIVE
PHYSIOLOGY.** By J. BURNEY YEO, M.B. Resident Medical Tutor and
Lecturer on Animal Physiology in King's College, London. [*Nearly ready.*

VAN DER HOEVEN'S HANDBOOK of ZOOLOGY. Translated from
the Second Dutch Edition by the Rev. W. CLARK, M.D. F.R.S. 2 vols. 8vo.
with 24 Plates of Figures, 60*s.*

Professor OWEN'S LECTURES on the COMPARATIVE ANATOMY
and Physiology of the Invertebrate Animals. Second Edition, with 235
Woodcuts. 8vo. 21*s.*

**The COMPARATIVE ANATOMY and PHYSIOLOGY of the VERTE-
brate Animals.** By RICHARD OWEN, F.R.S. D.C.L. With 1,472 Woodcuts. 3 vols. 8vo. £3 13*s.* 6*d.*

The ORIGIN of CIVILISATION and the PRIMITIVE CONDITION
of MAN; Mental and Social Condition of Savages. By Sir JOHN LUBBOCK,
Bart. M.P. F.R.S. With 25 Woodcuts. 8vo. price 16*s.*

The PRIMITIVE INHABITANTS of SCANDINAVIA: containing a
Description of the Implements, Dwellings, Tombs, and Mode of Living of
the Savages in the North of Europe during the Stone Age. By SVEN
NILSSON. With 16 Plates of Figures and 3 Woodcuts. 8vo. 18*s.*

BIBLE ANIMALS; being a Description of every Living Creature
mentioned in the Scriptures, from the Ape to the Coral. By the Rev. J. G.
WOOD, M.A. F.L.S. With about 100 Vignettes on Wood, 8vo. 21*s.*

HOMES WITHOUT HANDS: a Description of the Habitations of
Animals, classed according to their Principle of Construction. By Rev.
J. G. WOOD, M.A. F.L.S. With about 140 Vignettes on Wood, 8vo. 21*s.*

A FAMILIAR HISTORY of BIRDS. By E. STANLEY, D.D. F.R.S.
late Lord Bishop of Norwich. Seventh Edition, with Woodcuts. Fcp. 3*s.* 6*d.*

The **HARMONIES** of **NATURE** and **UNITY** of **CREATION**. By Dr. GEORGE HARTWIG. 8vo. with numerous Illustrations, 18s.

The **SEA** and its **LIVING WONDERS**. By the same Author. Third (English) Edition. 8vo. with many Illustrations, 21s.

The **TROPICAL WORLD**. By Dr. GEO. HARTWIG. With 8 Chromo-xylographs and 172 Woodcuts. 8vo. 21s.

The **POLAR WORLD**; a Popular Description of Man and Nature in the Arctic and Antarctic Regions of the Globe. By Dr. GEORGE HARTWIG. With 8 Chromoxylographs, 3 Maps, and 85 Woodcuts. 8vo. 21s.

KIRBY and **SPENCE'S INTRODUCTION** to **ENTOMOLOGY**, or Elements of the Natural History of Insects. 7th Edition. Crown 8vo. 5s.

MAUNDER'S TREASURY of **NATURAL HISTORY**, or Popular Dictionary of Zoology. Revised and corrected by T. S. COBBOLD, M.D. Fcp. with 900 Woodcuts, 6s. cloth, or 9s. 6d. bound in calf.

The **TREASURY** of **BOTANY**, or Popular Dictionary of the Vegetable Kingdom; including a Glossary of Botanical Terms. Edited by J. LINDLEY, F.R.S. and T. MOORE, F.L.S. assisted by eminent Contributors. With 274 Woodcuts and 20 Steel Plates. Two Parts, fcp. 12s. cloth, or 19s. calf.

The **ELEMENTS** of **BOTANY** for **FAMILIES** and **SCHOOLS**. Tenth Edition, revised by THOMAS MOORE, F.L.S. Fcp. with 154 Woodcuts, 2s. 6d.

The **ROSE AMATEUR'S GUIDE**. By THOMAS RIVERS. Ninth Edition. Fcp. 4s.

The **BRITISH FLORA**; comprising the Phænogamous or Flowering Plants and the Ferns. By Sir W. J. HOOKER, K.H. and G. A. WALKER-ARNOTT, LL.D. 12mo. with 12 Plates, 14s.

LOUDON'S ENCYCLOPÆDIA of **PLANTS**; comprising the Specific Character, Description, Culture, History, &c. of all the Plants found in Great Britain. With upwards of 12,000 Woodcuts. 8vo. 42s.

MAUNDER'S SCIENTIFIC and **LITERARY TREASURY**. New Edition, thoroughly revised and in great part re-written, with above 1,000 new Articles, by J. Y. JOHNSON, Corr. M.Z.S. Fcp. 6s. cloth, or 9s. 6d. calf.

A **DICTIONARY** of **SCIENCE, LITERATURE**, and **ART**. Fourth Edition, re-edited by W. T. BRANDE (the original Author), and GEORGE W. COX, M.A. assisted by contributors of eminent Scientific and Literary Acquirements. 3 vols. medium 8vo. price 63s. cloth.

Chemistry, Medicine, Surgery, and the Allied Sciences.

A **DICTIONARY** of **CHEMISTRY** and the Allied Branches of other Sciences. By HENRY WATTS, F.R.S. assisted by eminent Contributors. Complete in 5 vols. medium 8vo. £7 3s.

ELEMENTS of **CHEMISTRY**, Theoretical and Practical. By W. ALLEN MILLER, M.D. &c. Prof. of Chemistry, King's Coll. London. Fourth Edition. 3 vols. 8vo. £3. PART I. CHEMICAL PHYSICS, 15s. PART II. INORGANIC CHEMISTRY, 21s. PART III. ORGANIC CHEMISTRY, 24s.

A **MANUAL** of **CHEMISTRY**, Descriptive and Theoretical. By WILLIAM ODLING, M.B. F.R.S. PART I. 8vo. 9s. PART II. just ready.

OUTLINES of CHEMISTRY; or, Brief Notes of Chemical Facts. By WILLIAM ODLING, M.B. F.R.S. Crown 8vo. 7s. 6d.

A Course of Practical Chemistry, for the use of Medical Students. By the same Author. New Edition, with 70 Woodcuts. Crown 8vo. 7s. 6d.

Lectures on Animal Chemistry, delivered at the Royal College of Physicians in 1865. By the same Author. Crown 8vo. 4s. 6d.

LECTURES on the CHEMICAL CHANGES of CARBON. Delivered at the Royal Institution of Great Britain. By WILLIAM ODLING, M.B. F.R.S. Reprinted from the *Chemical News*, with Notes by W. CROOKES, F.R.S. Crown 8vo. price 4s. 6d.

HANDBOOK of CHEMICAL ANALYSIS, adapted to the UNITARY *System* of Notation. By F. T. CONINGTON, M.A. F.C.S. Post 8vo. 7s. 6d. —CONINGTON's *Tables of Qualitative Analysis*, price 2s. 6d.

A TREATISE on MEDICAL ELECTRICITY, THEORETICAL and PRACTICAL; and its Use in the Treatment of Paralysis, Neuralgia, and other Diseases. By JULIUS ALTHAUS, M.D. &c. Senior Physician to the Infirmary for Epilepsy and Paralysis. Second Edition, revised and partly re-written. Post 8vo. price 15s.

The DIAGNOSIS, PATHOLOGY, and TREATMENT of DISEASES of Women; including the Diagnosis of Pregnancy. By GRAILY HEWITT, M.D. Second Edition, enlarged; with 116 Woodcut Illustrations. 8vo. 24s.

LECTURES on the DISEASES of INFANCY and CHILDHOOD. By CHARLES WEST, M.D. &c. Fifth Edition, revised and enlarged. 8vo. 16s.

A SYSTEM of SURGERY, Theoretical and Practical. In Treatises by Various Authors. Edited by T. HOLMES, M.A. &c. Surgeon and Lecturer on Surgery at St. George's Hospital, and Surgeon-in-Chief to the Metropolitan Police. Second Edition, thoroughly revised, with numerous Illustrations. 5 vols. 8vo. £3 5s.

The SURGICAL TREATMENT of CHILDREN'S DISEASES. By T. HOLMES, M.A. &c. late Surgeon to the Hospital for Sick Children. Second Edition, with 9 Plates and 112 Woodcuts. 8vo. 21s.

LECTURES on the PRINCIPLES and PRACTICE of PHYSIC. By Sir THOMAS WATSON, Bart. M.D. New Edition in the press.

LECTURES on SURGICAL PATHOLOGY. By JAMES PAGET, F.R.S. Third Edition, revised and re-edited by the Author and Professor W. TURNER, M.B. 8vo. with 131 Woodcuts, 21s.

COOPER'S DICTIONARY of PRACTICAL SURGERY and Encyclopædia of Surgical Science. New Edition, brought down to the present time. By S. A. LANE, Surgeon to St. Mary's Hospital, assisted by various Eminent Surgeons. VOL. II. 8vo. completing the work. [*In the press.*

On CHRONIC BRONCHITIS, especially as connected with GOUT, EMPHYSEMA, and DISEASES of the HEART. By E. HEADLAM GREENHOW, M.D. F.R.C.P. &c. 8vo. 7s. 6d.

The CLIMATE of the SOUTH of FRANCE as SUITED to INVALIDS; with Notices of Mediterranean and other Winter Stations. By C. T. WILLIAMS, M.A. M.D. Oxon. Assistant-Physician to the Hospital for Consumption at Brompton. Second Edition, with Frontispiece and Map. Crown 8vo. 6s.

REPORTS on the PROGRESS of PRACTICAL and SCIENTIFIC MEDICINE in Different Parts of the World, from June 1868, to June 1869. Edited by HORACE DOBELL, M.D. assisted by numerous and distinguished Coadjutors. 8vo. 18s.

PULMONARY CONSUMPTION ; its Nature, Treatment, and Duration exemplified by an Analysis of One Thousand Cases selected from upwards of Twenty Thousand. By C. J. B. WILLIAMS, M.D. F.R.S. Consulting Physician to the Hospital for Consumption at Brompton; and C. T. WILLIAMS, M.A. M.D. Oxon. [*Nearly ready.*

CLINICAL LECTURES on DISEASES of the LIVER, JAUNDICE, and ABDOMINAL DROPSY. By CHARLES MURCHISON, M.D. Post 8vo. with 25 Woodcuts, 10s. 6d.

ANATOMY, DESCRIPTIVE and SURGICAL. By HENRY GRAY, F.R.S. With about 400 Woodcuts from Dissections. Fifth Edition, by T. HOLMES, M.A. Cantab. with a new Introduction by the Editor. Royal 8vo. 28s.

CLINICAL NOTES on DISEASES of the LARYNX, investigated and treated with the assistance of the Laryngoscope. By W. MARCET, M.D. F.R.S. Assistant-Physician to the Hospital for Consumption and Diseases of the Chest, Brompton. Crown 8vo. with 5 Lithographs, 6s.

The **THEORY of OCULAR DEFECTS and of SPECTACLES.** Translated from the German of Dr. H. SCHEFFLER by R. B. CARTER, F.R.C.S. With Prefatory Notes and a Chapter of Practical Instructions. Post 8vo. price 7s. 6d.

OUTLINES of PHYSIOLOGY, Human and Comparative. By JOHN MARSHALL, F.R.C.S. Surgeon to the University College Hospital. 2 vols. crown 8vo. with 122 Woodcuts, 32s.

ESSAYS on PHYSIOLOGICAL SUBJECTS. By GILBERT W. CHILD, M.A. Second Edition, revised, with Woodcuts. Crown 8vo. 7s. 6d.

PHYSIOLOGICAL ANATOMY and PHYSIOLOGY of MAN. By the late R. B. TODD, M.D. F.R.S. and W. BOWMAN, F.R.S. of King's College. With numerous Illustrations. VOL. II. 8vo. 25s.
VOL. I. New Edition by Dr. LIONEL S. BEALE, F.R.S. in course of publication; PART I. with 8 Plates, 7s. 6d.

COPLAND'S DICTIONARY of PRACTICAL MEDICINE, abridged from the larger work and throughout brought down to the present State of Medical Science. 8vo. 36s.

REIMANN'S HANDBOOK of ANILINE and its DERIVATIVES; a Treatise on the Manufacture of Aniline and Aniline Colours. Edited by WILLIAM CROOKES, F.R.S. With 5 Woodcuts. 8vo. 10s. 6d.

A **MANUAL of MATERIA MEDICA and THERAPEUTICS,** abridged from Dr. PEREIRA's *Elements* by F. J. FARRE, M.D. assisted by R. BENTLEY, M.R.C.S. and by R. WARINGTON, F.R.S. 8vo. with 90 Woodcuts, 21s.

THOMSON'S CONSPECTUS of the BRITISH PHARMACOPŒIA. 25th Edition, corrected by E. LLOYD BIRKETT, M.D. 18mo. price 6s.

MANUAL of the DOMESTIC PRACTICE of MEDICINE. By W. B. KESTEVEN, F.R.C.S.E. Third Edition, revised, with Additions. Fcp. 5s.

GYMNASTS and GYMNASTICS. By JOHN H. HOWARD, late Professor of Gymnastics, Comm. Coll. Ripponden. Second Edition, revised and enlarged, with 135 Woodcuts. Crown 8vo. 10s. 6d.

The Fine Arts, and *Illustrated Editions.*

IN FAIRYLAND; Pictures from the Elf-World. By RICHARD DOYLE. With a Poem by W. ALLINGHAM. With Sixteen Plates, containing Thirty-six Designs printed in Colours. Folio, 31s. 6d.

LIFE of JOHN GIBSON, R.A. SCULPTOR.   Edited by Lady EASTLAKE. 8vo. 10s. 6d.

The LORD'S PRAYER ILLUSTRATED by F. R. PICKERSGILL, R.A. and HENRY ALFORD, D.D. Dean of Canterbury. Imp. 4to. price 21s. cloth.

MATERIALS for a HISTORY of OIL PAINTING. By Sir CHARLES LOCKE EASTLAKE, sometime President of the Royal Academy. 2 vols. 8vo. price 30s.

HALF-HOUR LECTURES on the HISTORY and PRACTICE of the Fine and Ornamental Arts. By WILLIAM B. SCOTT. New Edition, revised by the Author; with 50 Woodcuts. Crown 8vo. 8s. 6d.

ALBERT DURER, HIS LIFE and WORKS; including Auto-biographical Papers and Complete Catalogues. By WILLIAM B. SCOTT. With Six Etchings by the Author, and other Illustrations. 8vo. 16s.

SIX LECTURES on HARMONY, delivered at the Royal Institution of Great Britain in the Year 1867. By G. A. MACFARREN. With numerous engraved Musical Examples and Specimens. 8vo. 10s. 6d.

The CHORALE BOOK for ENGLAND: the Hymns translated by Miss C. WINKWORTH; the tunes arranged by Prof. W. S. BENNETT and OTTO GOLDSCHMIDT. Fcp. 4to. 12s. 6d.

The NEW TESTAMENT, illustrated with Wood Engravings after the Early Masters, chiefly of the Italian School. Crown 4to. 63s. cloth, gilt top; or £5 5s. elegantly bound in morocco.

LYRA GERMANICA; the Christian Year. Translated by CATHERINE WINKWORTH; with 125 Illustrations on Wood drawn by J. LEIGHTON, F.S.A. 4to. 21s.

LYRA GERMANICA; the Christian Life. Translated by CATHERINE WINKWORTH; with about 200 Woodcut Illustrations by J. LEIGHTON, F.S.A. and other Artists. 4to. 21s.

The LIFE of MAN SYMBOLISED by the MONTHS of the YEAR. Text selected by R. PIGOT; Illustrations on Wood from Original Designs by J. LEIGHTON, F.S.A. 4to. 42s.

CATS' and FARLIE'S MORAL EMBLEMS; with Aphorisms, Adages, and Proverbs of all Nations. 121 Illustrations on Wood by J. LEIGHTON, F.S.A. Text selected by R. PIGOT. Imperial 8vo. 31s. 6d.

SHAKSPEARE'S MIDSUMMER-NIGHT'S DREAM, illustrated with 24 Silhouettes or Shadow-Pictures by P. KONEWKA, engraved on Wood by A. VOGEL. Folio, 31s. 6d.

SHAKSPEARE'S SENTIMENTS and SIMILES, printed in Black and Gold, and Illuminated in the Missal Style by HENRY NOEL HUMPHREYS. Square post 8vo. 21s.

SACRED and **LEGENDARY ART.** By Mrs. JAMESON.

Legends of the Saints and Martyrs. Fifth Edition, with 19 Etchings and 187 Woodcuts. 2 vols. square crown 8vo. 31s. 6d.

Legends of the Monastic Orders. Third Edition, with 11 Etchings and 88 Woodcuts. 1 vol. square crown 8vo. 21s.

Legends of the Madonna. Third Edition, with 27 Etchings and 165 Woodcuts. 1 vol. square crown 8vo. 21s.

The History of Our Lord, with that of his Types and Precursors. Completed by Lady EASTLAKE. Revised Edition, with 31 Etchings and 281 Woodcuts. 2 vols. square crown 8vo. 42s.

The Useful Arts, Manufactures, &c.

HISTORY of the **GOTHIC REVIVAL**; an Attempt to shew how far the taste for Mediæval Architecture was retained in England during the last two centuries, and has been re-developed in the present. By CHARLES L. EASTLAKE, Architect. With many Illustrations. [*Nearly ready.*]

GWILT'S ENCYCLOPÆDIA of ARCHITECTURE, with above 1,100 Engravings on Wood. Fifth Edition, revised and enlarged by WYATT PAPWORTH. Additionally illustrated with nearly 400 Wood Engravings by O. Jewitt, and more than 100 other new Woodcuts. 8vo. 52s. 6d.

ITALIAN SCULPTORS; being a History of Sculpture in Northern, Southern, and Eastern Italy. By C. C. PERKINS. With 30 Etchings and 13 Wood Engravings. Imperial 8vo. 42s.

TUSCAN SCULPTORS, their Lives, Works, and Times. With 45 Etchings and 28 Woodcuts from Original Drawings and Photographs. By the same Author. 2 vols. imperial 8vo. 63s.

HINTS on **HOUSEHOLD TASTE** in **FURNITURE, UPHOLSTERY,** and other Details. By CHARLES L. EASTLAKE, Architect. Second Edition, with about 90 Illustrations. Square crown 8vo. 18s.

The ENGINEER'S HANDBOOK; explaining the Principles which should guide the Young Engineer in the Construction of Machinery. By C. S. LOWNDES. Post 8vo. 5s.

PRINCIPLES of MECHANISM, designed for the Use of Students in the Universities, and for Engineering Students generally. By R. WILLIS, M.A. F.R.S. &c. Jacksonian Professor in the University of Cambridge. A new and enlarged Edition. 8vo. [*Nearly ready.*]

LATHES and **TURNING,** Simple, Mechanical, and **ORNAMENTAL.** By W. HENRY NORTHCOTT. With about 240 Illustrations on Steel and Wood. 8vo. 18s.

URE'S DICTIONARY of ARTS, MANUFACTURES, and **MINES.** Sixth Edition, chiefly rewritten and greatly enlarged by ROBERT HUNT, F.R.S. assisted by numerous Contributors eminent in Science and the Arts, and familiar with Manufactures. With above 2,000 Woodcuts. 3 vols. medium 8vo. price £4 14s. 6d.

HANDBOOK of PRACTICAL TELEGRAPHY, published with the sanction of the Chairman and Directors of the Electric and International Telegraph Company, and adopted by the Department of Telegraphs for India. By R. S. CULLEY. Third Edition. 8vo. 12s. 6d.

C

ENCYCLOPÆDIA of CIVIL ENGINEERING, Historical, Theoretical, and Practical. By E. CRESY, C.E. With above 3,000 Woodcuts. 8vo. 42s.

TREATISE on MILLS and MILLWORK. By Sir W. FAIRBAIRN, F.R.S. Second Edition, with 18 Plates and 322 Woodcuts. 2 vols. 8vo. 32s.

USEFUL INFORMATION for ENGINEERS. By the same Author. FIRST, SECOND, and THIRD SERIES, with many Plates and Woodcuts. 3 vols. crown 8vo. 10s. 6d. each.

The APPLICATION of CAST and WROUGHT IRON to Building Purposes. By the same Author. Fourth Edition, enlarged; with 6 Plates and 118 Woodcuts. 8vo. price 16s.

. IRON SHIP BUILDING, its History and Progress, as comprised in a Series of Experimental Researches. By the same Author. With 4 Plates and 130 Woodcuts. 8vo. 18s.

A TREATISE on the STEAM ENGINE, in its various Applications to Mines, Mills, Steam Navigation, Railways and Agriculture. By J. BOURNE, C.E. Eighth Edition; with Portrait, 37 Plates, and 546 Woodcuts. 4to. 42s.

CATECHISM of the STEAM ENGINE, in its various Applications to Mines, Mills, Steam Navigation, Railways, and Agriculture. By the same Author. With 89 Woodcuts. Fcp. 6s.

HANDBOOK of the STEAM ENGINE. By the same Author, forming a KEY to the Catechism of the Steam Engine, with 67 Woodcuts. Fcp. 9s.

BOURNE'S RECENT IMPROVEMENTS in the STEAM ENGINE in its various applications to Mines, Mills, Steam Navigation, Railways, and Agriculture. Being a Supplement to the Author's 'Catechism of the Steam Engine.' By JOHN BOURNE. C.E. New Edition, including many New Examples; with 124 Woodcuts. Fcp. 8vo. 6s.

A TREATISE on the SCREW PROPELLER, SCREW VESSELS, and Screw Engines, as adapted for purposes of Peace and War; with Notices of other Methods of Propulsion, Tables of the Dimensions and Performance of Screw Steamers, and detailed Specifications of Ships and Engines. By J. BOURNE, C.E. New Edition, with 54 Plates and 287 Woodcuts. 4to. 63s. .

EXAMPLES of MODERN STEAM, AIR, and GAS ENGINES of the most Approved Types, as employed for Pumping, for Driving Machinery, for Locomotion, and for Agriculture, minutely and practically described. By JOHN BOURNE, C.E. In course of publication in 24 Parts, price 2s. 6d. each, forming One volume 4to. with about 50 Plates and 400 Woodcuts.

A HISTORY of the MACHINE-WROUGHT HOSIERY and LACE Manufactures. By WILLIAM FELKIN, F.L.S. F.S.S. Royal 8vo. 21s.

PRACTICAL TREATISE on METALLURGY, adapted from the last German Edition of Professor KERL'S Metallurgy by W. CROOKES, F.R.S. &c. and E. RÖHRIG, Ph.D. M.E. In Three Volumes, 8vo. with 625 Woodcuts. VOL. I. price 31s. 6d. VOL. II. price 36s. VOL. III. price 31s. 6d.

MITCHELL'S MANUAL of PRACTICAL ASSAYING. Third Edition, for the most part re-written, with all the recent Discoveries incorporated, by W. CROOKES, F.R.S. With 188 Woodcuts. 8vo. 28s.

The ART of PERFUMERY; the History and Theory of Odours, and the Methods of Extracting the Aromas of Plants. By Dr. PIESSE, F.C.S. Third Edition, with 53 Woodcuts. Crown 8vo. 10s. 6d.

Chemical, Natural, and Physical Magic, for Juveniles during the Holidays. By the same Author. Third Edition, with 38 Woodcuts. Fcp. 6s.

LOUDON'S ENCYCLOPÆDIA of AGRICULTURE: comprising the Laying-out, Improvement, and Management of Landed Property, and the Cultivation and Economy of the Productions of Agriculture. With 1,100 Woodcuts. 8vo. 21s.

Loudon's Encyclopædia of Gardening: comprising the Theory and Practice of Horticulture, Floriculture, Arboriculture, and Landscape Gardening. With 1,000 Woodcuts. 8vo. 21s.

BAYLDON'S ART of VALUING RENTS and TILLAGES, and Claims of Tenants upon Quitting Farms, both at Michaelmas and Lady-Day. Eighth Edition, revised by J. C. MORTON. 8vo. 10s. 6d.

Religious and *Moral Works.*

CONSIDERATIONS on the REVISION of the ENGLISH NEW TESTAMENT. By C. J. ELLICOTT, D.D. Lord Bishop of Gloucester and Bristol. Post 8vo. price 5s. 6d.

An EXPOSITION of the 39 ARTICLES, Historical and Doctrinal. By E. HAROLD BROWNE, D.D. Lord Bishop of Ely. Seventh Edit. 8vo. 16s.

BISHOP COTTON'S INSTRUCTIONS in the PRINCIPLES and Practice of Christianity, intended chiefly as an introduction to Confirmation. Sixth Edition, 18mo. 2s. 6d.

The ACTS of the APOSTLES; with a Commentary, and Practical and Devotional Suggestions for Readers and Students of the English Bible. By the Rev. F. C. COOK, M.A. Canon of Exeter, &c. New Edition. 8vo. 12s. 6d.

The LIFE and EPISTLES of ST. PAUL. By the Rev. W. J. CONYBEARE, M.A., and the Very Rev. J. S. HOWSON, D.D. Dean of Chester:—
LIBRARY EDITION, with all the Original Illustrations, Maps, Landscapes on Steel, Woodcuts, &c. 2 vols. 4to. 48s.
INTERMEDIATE EDITION, with a Selection of Maps, Plates, and Woodcuts. 2 vols. square crown 8vo. 31s. 6d.
STUDENT'S EDITION, revised and condensed, with 46 Illustrations and Maps. 1 vol. crown 8vo. price 9s.

The VOYAGE and SHIPWRECK of ST. PAUL; with Dissertations on the Life and Writings of St. Luke and the Ships and Navigation of the Ancients. By JAMES SMITH, F.R.S. Third Edition. Crown 8vo. 10s. 6d.

A CRITICAL and GRAMMATICAL COMMENTARY on ST. PAUL'S Epistles. By C. J. ELLICOTT, D.D. Lord Bishop of Gloucester & Bristol. 8vo.

Galatians, Fourth Edition, 8s. 6d.

Ephesians, Fourth Edition, 8s. 6d.

Pastoral Epistles, Fourth Edition, 10s. 6d.

Philippians, Colossians, and Philemon, Third Edition, 10s. 6d.

Thessalonians, Third Edition, 7s. 6d.

HISTORICAL LECTURES on the LIFE of OUR LORD JESUS CHRIST: being the Hulsean Lectures for 1859. By C. J. ELLICOTT, D.D. Lord Bishop of Gloucester and Bristol. Fifth Edition. 8vo. price 12s.

'SPIRITUAL SONGS' for the SUNDAYS and HOLIDAYS throughout the Year. By J. S. B. MONSELL, LL.D. Vicar of Egham and Rural Dean. Fourth Edition, Sixth Thousand. Fcp. 4s. 6d.

The BEATITUDES: Abasement before God; Sorrow for Sin; Meekness of Spirit; Desire for Holiness; Gentleness; Purity of Heart; the Peacemakers; Sufferings for Christ. By the same. Third Edition. Fcp. 3s. 6d.

His PRESENCE—not his MEMORY, 1855. By the same Author, in Memory of his Son. Sixth Edition. 16mo. 1s.

LYRA EUCHARISTICA; Hymns and Verses on the Holy Communion, Ancient and Modern: with other Poems. Edited by the Rev. ORBY SHIPLEY, M.A. Second Edition. Fcp. 5s.

Lyra Messianica; Hymns and Verses on the Life of Christ, Ancient and Modern; with other Poems. By the same Editor. Second Edition, altered and enlarged. Fcp. 5s.

Lyra Mystica; Hymns and Verses on Sacred Subjects, Ancient and Modern. By the same Editor. Fcp. 5s.

ENDEAVOURS after the CHRISTIAN LIFE: Discourses. By JAMES MARTINEAU. Fourth and cheaper Edition, carefully revised; the Two Series complete in One Volume. Post 8vo. 7s. 6d.

INVOCATION of SAINTS and ANGELS, for the use of Members of the English Church. Edited by the Rev. ORBY SHIPLEY. 24mo. 3s. 6d.

WHATELY'S INTRODUCTORY LESSONS on the CHRISTIAN Evidences. 18mo. 6d.

WHATELY'S INTRODUCTORY LESSONS on the HISTORY of Religious Worship. New Edition. 18mo. 2s. 6d.

BISHOP JEREMY TAYLOR'S ENTIRE WORKS. With Life by BISHOP HEBER. Revised and corrected by the Rev. C. P. EDEN, 10 vols. price £5 5s.

Travels, Voyages, &c.

NARRATIVE of a SPRING TOUR in PORTUGAL. By A. C. SMITH, M.A. Ch. Ch. Oxon. Rector of Yatesbury. Post 8vo. price 6s. 6d.

ENGLAND to DELHI; a Narrative of Indian Travel. By JOHN MATHESON, Glasgow. With Map and 82 Woodcut Illustrations. 4to. 31s. 6d.

CADORE; or, TITIAN'S COUNTRY. By JOSIAH GILBERT, one of the Authors of 'The Dolomite Mountains.' With Map, Facsimile, and 40 Illustrations. Imperial 8vo. 31s. 6d.

NARRATIVE of the EUPHRATES EXPEDITION carried on by Order of the British Government during the years 1835–1837. By General F. R. CHESNEY, F.R.S. With Maps, Plates, and Woodcuts. 8vo. 24s.

TRAVELS in the CENTRAL CAUCASUS and BASHAN. Including Visits to Ararat and Tabreez and Ascents of Kazbek and Elbruz. By D. W. FRESHFIELD. Square crown 8vo. with Maps, &c. 18s.

PICTURES in TYROL and Elsewhere. From a Family Sketch-Book. By the Authoress of 'A Voyage en Zigzag,' &c. Second Edition. Small 4to. with numerous Illustrations, 21s.

HOW WE SPENT the SUMMER; or, a Voyage en Zigzag in Switzerland and Tyrol with some Members of the ALPINE CLUB. From the Sketch-Book of one of the Party. In oblong 4to. with 300 Illustrations, 15s.

BEATEN TRACKS; or, Pen and Pencil Sketches in Italy. By the Authoress of 'A Voyage en Zigzag.' With 42 Plates, containing about 200 Sketches from Drawings made on the Spot. 8vo. 16s.

MAP of the **CHAIN** of **MONT BLANC**, from an actual Survey in 1863—1864. By A. ADAMS-REILLY, F.R.G.S. M.A.C. Published under the Authority of the Alpine Club. In Chromolithography on extra stout drawing-paper 28in. × 17in. price 10s. or mounted on canvas in a folding case, 12s. 6d.

WESTWARD by **RAIL**; the New Route to the East. By W. F. RAE. With Map shewing the Lines of Rail between the Atlantic and the Pacific, and Sections of the Railway. Post 8vo. price 10s. 6d.

The **PARAGUAYAN WAR**: with Sketches of the History of Paraguay, and of the Manners and Customs of the People; and Notes on the Military Engineering of the War. By GEORGE THOMPSON, C.E. With 8 Maps and Plans, and a Portrait of Lopez. Post 8vo. 12s. 6d.

HISTORY of **DISCOVERY** in our **AUSTRALASIAN COLONIES**, Australia, Tasmania, and New Zealand, from the Earliest Date to the Present Day. By WILLIAM HOWITT. 2 vols. 8vo. with 3 Maps, 20s.

NOTES on **BURGUNDY**. By CHARLES RICHARD WELD. Edited by his Widow; with Portrait and Memoir. Post 8vo. 8s. 6d.

The **CAPITAL** of the **TYCOON**; a Narrative of a Three Years' Residence in Japan. By Sir RUTHERFORD ALCOCK, K.C.B. 2 vols. 8vo. with numerous Illustrations, 42s.

The **DOLOMITE MOUNTAINS**; Excursions through Tyrol, Carinthia, Carniola, and Friuli, 1861-1863. By J. GILBERT and G. C. CHURCHILL, F.R.G.S. With numerous Illustrations. Square crown 8vo. 21s.

GUIDE to the **PYRENEES**, for the use of Mountaineers. By CHARLES PACKE. 2nd Edition, with Map and Illustrations. Cr. 8vo. 7s. 6d.

The **ALPINE GUIDE**. By JOHN BALL, M.R.I.A. late President of the Alpine Club. Thoroughly Revised Editions, in Three Volumes, post 8vo. with Maps and other Illustrations:—

GUIDE to the **WESTERN ALPS**, including Mont Blanc, Monte Rosa, Zermatt, &c. Price 6s. 6d.

GUIDE to the **CENTRAL ALPS**, including all the Oberland District. 7s. 6d.

GUIDE to the **EASTERN ALPS**, price 10s. 6d.

Introduction on Alpine Travelling in General, and on the Geology of the Alps, price 1s. Each of the Three Volumes or Parts of the *Alpine Guide* may be had with this INTRODUCTION prefixed, price 1s. extra.

The **HIGH ALPS WITHOUT GUIDES**. By the Rev. A. G. GIRDLESTONE, M.A. late Demy in Natural Science, Magdalen College, Oxford. With Frontispiece and 2 Maps. Square crown 8vo. price 7s. 6d.

MEMORIALS of **LONDON** and **LONDON LIFE** in the 13th, 14th, and 15th Centuries; being a Series of Extracts, Local, Social, and Political, from the Archives of the City of London, A.D. 1276-1419. Selected, translated, and edited by H. T. RILEY, M.A. Royal 8vo. 21s.

COMMENTARIES on the **HISTORY, CONSTITUTION**, and **CHARTERED FRANCHISES** of the CITY of LONDON. By GEORGE NORTON, formerly one of the Common Pleaders of the City of London. Third Edition. 8vo. 14s.

The **NORTHERN HEIGHTS** of **LONDON**; or, Historical Associations of Hampstead, Highgate, Muswell Hill, Hornsey, and Islington. By WILLIAM HOWITT. With about 40 Woodcuts. Square crown 8vo. 21s.

VISITS to **REMARKABLE PLACES**: Old Halls, Battle-Fields, and Scenes Illustrative of Striking Passages in English History and Poetry. By WILLIAM HOWITT. 2 vols. square crown 8vo. with Woodcuts, 25s.

The **RURAL LIFE** of **ENGLAND**. By the same Author. With Woodcuts by Bewick and Williams. Medium 8vo. 12s. 6d.

ROMA SOTTERRANEA; or, an Account of the Roman Catacombs, especially of the Cemetery of San Callisto. Compiled from the Works of Commendatore G. B. De Rossi by the Rev. J. S. NORTHCOTE, D.D. and the Rev. W. R. BROWNLOW. With numerous Illustrations. 8vo. 31s. 6d.

PILGRIMAGES in the **PYRENEES and LANDES**. By DENYS SHYNE LAWLOR. Crown 8vo. with Frontispiece and Vignette, price 15s.

The **GERMAN WORKING MAN**; being an Account of the Daily Life, Amusements, and Unions for Culture and Material Progress of the Artisans of North and South Germany and Switzerland. By JAMES SAMUELSON. Crown 8vo. with Frontispiece, 3s. 6d.

Works of Fiction.

LOTHAIR. By the Right Hon. B. DISRAELI, M.P. Seventh Edition. 3 vols. post 8vo. price 31s. 6d.
> Nôsse omnia hæc, salus est adolescentulis.—TERENTIUS.

NO APPEAL; a Novel. By the Author of 'Cut down like Grass.' 3 vols. post 8vo. price 31s. 6d.

The **MODERN NOVELIST'S LIBRARY.** Each Work, in crown 8vo. complete in a Single Volume:—
MELVILLE'S GLADIATORS. 2s. boards; 2s. 6d. cloth.
———— HOLMBY HOUSE, 2s. boards; 2s. 6d. cloth.
———— INTERPRETER, 2s. boards; 2s. 6d. cloth.
TROLLOPE'S WARDEN, 1s. 6d. boards; 2s. cloth.
———— BARCHESTER TOWERS, 2s. boards; 2s. 6d. cloth.
BRAMLEY-MOORE'S SIX SISTERS OF THE VALLEYS, 2s. boards; 2s. 6d. cloth.

THREE WEDDINGS. By the Author of 'Dorothy,' 'De Cressy,' &c. Fcp. 8vo. price 5s.

STORIES and **TALES** by ELIZABETH M. SEWELL, Author of 'Amy Herbert,' uniform Edition, each Story or Tale complete in a single Volume:
AMY HERBERT, 2s. 6d.
GERTRUDE, 2s. 6d.
EARL'S DAUGHTER, 2s. 6d.
EXPERIENCE OF LIFE, 2s. 6d.
CLEVE HALL, 3s. 6d.
IVORS, 3s. 6d.
KATHARINE ASHTON, 3s. 6d.
MARGARET PERCIVAL, 5s.
LANETON PARSONAGE, 4s. 6d.
URSULA, 4s. 6d.

A Glimpse of the World. By the Author of 'Amy Herbert.' Fcp. 7s. 6d.

The Journal of a Home Life. By the same Author. Post 8vo. 9s. 6d.

After Life; a Sequel to 'The Journal of a Home Life.' Price 10s. 6d.

UNCLE PETER'S FAIRY TALE for the **XIX CENTURY.** Edited by E. M. SEWELL, Author of 'Amy Herbert,' &c. Fcp. 8vo. 7s. 6d.

VIKRAM and the **VAMPIRE**; or, Tales of Hindu Devilry. Adapted by RICHARD F. BURTON, F.R.G.S. &c. With 33 Illustrations by Ernest Griset. Crown 8vo. 9s.

THROUGH the NIGHT; a Tale of the Times. To which is added
'Onward, or a Summer Sketch.' By WALTER SWEETMAN, B.A. 2 vols. post
8vo. 21s.

BECKER'S GALLUS; or, Roman Scenes of the Time of Augustus:
with Notes and Excursuses. New Edition. Post 8vo. 7s. 6d.

BECKER'S CHARICLES; a Tale illustrative of Private Life among the
Ancient Greeks: with Notes and Excursuses. New Edition. Post 8vo. 7s. 6d.

NOVELS and TALES by G. J. WHYTE MELVILLE :—

The GLADIATORS, 5s.	HOLMBY HOUSE, 5s.
DIGBY GRAND, 5s.	GOOD for NOTHING, 6s.
KATE COVENTRY, 5s.	The QUEEN'S MARIES, 6s.
GENERAL BOUNCE, 5s.	The INTERPRETER, 5s.

TALES of ANCIENT GREECE. By GEORGE W. COX, M.A. late
Scholar of Trin. Coll. Oxon. Being a Collective Edition of the Author's
Classical Stories and Tales, complete in One Volume. Crown 8vo. 6s. 6d.

A MANUAL of MYTHOLOGY, in the form of Question and Answer.
By the same Author. Fcp. 3s.

OUR CHILDREN'S STORY, by one of their Gossips. By the Author
of 'Voyage en Zigzag,' 'Pictures in Tyrol,' &c. Small 4to. with Sixty Illustrations by the Author, price 10s. 6d.

Poetry and The Drama.

THOMAS MOORE'S POETICAL WORKS, the only Editions contain-
ing the Author's last Copyright Additions :—
CABINET EDITION, 10 vols. fcp. 8vo. price 35s.
SHAMROCK EDITION, crown 8vo. price 3s. 6d.
RUBY EDITION, crown 8vo. with Portrait, price 6s.
LIBRARY EDITION, medium 8vo. Portrait and Vignette, 14s.
PEOPLE'S EDITION, square crown 8vo. with Portrait, &c. 10s. 6d.

MOORE'S IRISH MELODIES, Maclise's Edition, with 161 Steel Plates
from Original Drawings. Super-royal 8vo. 31s. 6d.

Miniature Edition of Moore's Irish Melodies with Maclise's Designs (as above) reduced in Lithography. Imp. 16mo. 10s. 6d.

MOORE'S LALLA ROOKH. Tenniel's Edition, with 68 Wood
Engravings from original Drawings and other Illustrations. Fcp. 4to. 21s.

SOUTHEY'S POETICAL WORKS, with the Author's last Corrections
and copyright Additions. Library Edition, in 1 vol. medium 8vo. with
Portrait and Vignette, 14s.

LAYS of ANCIENT ROME; with Ivry and the Armada. By the
Right Hon. LORD MACAULAY. 16mo. 4s. 6d.

Lord Macaulay's Lays of Ancient Rome. With 90 Illustrations on
Wood, from the Antique, from Drawings by G. SCHARF. Fcp. 4to. 21s.

Miniature Edition of Lord Macaulay's Lays of Ancient Rome,
with the Illustrations (as above) reduced in Lithography. Imp. 16mo. 10s. 6d.

GOLDSMITH'S POETICAL WORKS, with Wood Engravings from
Designs by Members of the ETCHING CLUB. Imperial 16mo. 7s. 6d.

POEMS. By JEAN INGELOW. Fifteenth Edition. Fcp. 8vo. 5s.

POEMS by Jean Ingelow. With nearly 100 Illustrations by Eminent
Artists, engraved on Wood by the Brothers DALZIEL. Fcp. 4to. 21s.

B

MOPSA the FAIRY. By JEAN INGELOW.   Pp. 256, with Eight Illustrations engraved on Wood. Fcp. 8vo. 6s.

A STORY of DOOM, and other Poems. By JEAN INGELOW.   Third Edition. Fcp. 5s.

POETICAL WORKS of LETITIA ELIZABETH LANDON (L.E.L.). 2 vols. 16mo. 10s.

GLAPHYRA, and OTHER POEMS By FRANCIS REYNOLDS, Author of 'Alice Rushton, and other Poems.' 16mo. price 5s.

BOWDLER'S FAMILY SHAKSPEARE, cheaper Genuine Editions: Medium 8vo. large type, with 36 Woodcuts, price 14s. Cabinet Edition, with the same ILLUSTRATIONS, 6 vols. fcp. 3s. 6d. each.

HORATII OPERA, Pocket Edition, with carefully corrected Text, Marginal References, and Introduction.   Edited by the Rev. J. E. YONGE, M.A.   Square 18mo. 4s. 6d.

HORATII OPERA. Library Edition, with Marginal References and English Notes. Edited by the Rev. J. E. YONGE. 8vo. 21s.

The ÆNEID of VIRGIL Translated into English Verse. By JOHN CONINGTON, M.A. New Edition. Crown 8vo. 9s.

ARUNDINES CAMI, sive Musarum Cantabrigiensium Lusus canori. Collegit atque edidit H. DRURY, M.A. Editio Sexta, curavit H. J. HODGSON, M.A. Crown 8vo. 7s. 6d.

HUNTING SONGS and MISCELLANEOUS VERSES. By R. E. EGERTON WARBURTON. Second Edition. Fcp. 8vo. 5s.

The SILVER STORE collected from Mediæval Christian and Jewish Mines. By the Rev. SABINE BARING-GOULD, M.A. Crown 8vo. 3s. 6d.

Rural Sports, &c.

ENCYCLOPÆDIA of RURAL SPORTS; a complete Account, Historical, Practical, and Descriptive, of Hunting, Shooting, Fishing, Racing, and all other Rural and Athletic Sports and Pastimes. By D. P. BLAINE. With above 600 Woodcuts (20 from Designs by JOHN LEECH). 8vo. 21s.

Col. HAWKER'S INSTRUCTIONS to YOUNG SPORTSMEN in all that relates to Guns and Shooting. Revised by the Author's Son. Square crown 8vo. with Illustrations, 18s.

The DEAD SHOT, or Sportsman's Complete Guide; a Treatise on the Use of the Gun, Dog-breaking, Pigeon-shooting, &c. By MARKSMAN. Revised Edition. Fcp. 8vo. with Plates, 5s.

The FLY-FISHER'S ENTOMOLOGY. By ALFRED RONALDS. With coloured Representations of the Natural and Artificial Insect. Sixth Edition; with 20 coloured Plates. 8vo. 14s.

A BOOK on ANGLING; a complete Treatise on the Art of Angling in every branch. By FRANCIS FRANCIS. Second Edition, with Portrait and 15 other Plates, plain and coloured. Post 8vo. 15s.

The BOOK of the ROACH. By GREVILLE FENNELL, of 'The Field.' Fcp. 8vo. price 2s. 6d.

WILCOCKS'S SEA-FISHERMAN; comprising the Chief Methods of Hook and Line Fishing in the British and other Seas, a Glance at Nets, and Remarks on Boats and Boating. Second Edition, enlarged; with 80 Woodcuts. Post 8vo. 12s. 6d.

HORSES and STABLES. By Colonel F. FITZWYGRAM, XV. the King's Hussars. With Twenty-four Plates of Illustrations, containing very numerous Figures engraved on Wood. 8vo. 15s.

The HORSE'S FOOT, and HOW to KEEP IT SOUND. By W. MILES, Esq. Ninth Edition, with Illustrations. Imperial 8vo. 12s. 6d.

A PLAIN TREATISE on HORSE-SHOEING. By the same Author. Sixth Edition. Post 8vo. with Illustrations, 2s. 6d.

STABLES and STABLE-FITTINGS. By the same. Imp. 8vo. with 13 Plates, 15s.

REMARKS on HORSES' TEETH, addressed to Purchasers. By the same. Post 8vo. 1s. 6d.

ROBBINS'S CAVALRY CATECHISM, or Instructions on Cavalry Exercise and Field Movements, Brigade Movements, Out-post Duty, Cavalry supporting Artillery, Artillery attached to Cavalry. 12mo. 5s.

BLAINE'S VETERINARY ART; a Treatise on the Anatomy, Physiology, and Curative Treatment of the Diseases of the Horse, Neat Cattle and Sheep. Seventh Edition, revised and enlarged by C. STEEL, M.R.C.V.S.L. 8vo. with Plates and Woodcuts. 18s.

The HORSE: with a Treatise on Draught. By WILLIAM YOUATT. New Edition, revised and enlarged. 8vo. with numerous Woodcuts, 12s. 6d.

The Dog. By the same Author. 8vo. with numerous Woodcuts, 6s.

The DOG in HEALTH and DISEASE. By STONEHENGE. With 70 Wood Engravings. Square crown 8vo. 10s. 6d.

The GREYHOUND. By STONEHENGE. Revised Edition, with 24 Portraits of Greyhounds. Square crown 8vo. 10s. 6d.

The OX; his Diseases and their Treatment: with an Essay on Parturition in the Cow. By J. R. DOBSON. Crown 8vo. with Illustrations. 7s. 6d.

Commerce, Navigation, and Mercantile Affairs.

The ELEMENTS of BANKING. By HENRY DUNNING MACLEOD, M.A. Barrister-at-Law. Post 8vo. [*Nearly ready.*

The THEORY and PRACTICE of BANKING. By the same Author. Second Edition, entirely remodelled. 2 vols. 8vo. 30s.

PRACTICAL GUIDE for BRITISH SHIPMASTERS to UNITED States Ports. By PIERREPONT EDWARDS. Post 8vo. 8s. 6d.

A DICTIONARY, Practical, Theoretical, and Historical, of Commerce and Commercial Navigation. By J. R. M'CULLOCH, Esq. New and thoroughly revised Edition. 8vo. price 63s. cloth, or 70s. half-bd. in russia.

The LAW of NATIONS Considered as Independent Political Communities. By Sir TRAVERS TWISS, D.C.L. 2 vols. 8vo. 30s., or separately, PART I. *Peace*, 12s. PART II. *War*, 18s.